美國的國際詩人會頒給沙白的詩「化粧（Cosmetics）」卓越獎

沙白（涂秀田）1995年榮獲國際詩人獎

星星亮晶晶
Twinkle, Twinkle, Little Stars

著・沙 白 Sar Po
譯・陳靖奇教授 Prof Ching-chi Chen, Ph.d.
圖・童錦茂

目錄

黃榮村序（考試院院長／前中國醫藥大學校長） Foreword-By 6

毛連塭局長序 Foreword-By Mao Lianwen 8

苗栗縣長徐耀昌 Foreword-By Yao-chang Hsu 10

南投縣長林明溱 Mingzhen Lin 12

澎湖縣長賴峰偉 Feng-wui Lai 14

林良理事長序 Foreword by Lin Liang 16

林煥彰序 Lin Huanzhang 22

自序 Preface 26

太陽 The Sun 30

月亮 The Moon 32

小星星 Little Stars 34

春風 Spring Breezes 36

海風 Sea Breezes 38

颱風 A Typhoon 40

雪 Snow 42

瀑布 Waterfalls 44

雨 Rain 46

雲 The Clouds	48
閃電 Lightning	50
雷 Thunder	52
春天 Spring	54
夏天 Summer	56
秋天 Autumn	58
冬天 Winter	60
白天 Daytime	62
黃昏 Dusk	64
黑夜 Black Night	66
露 Dew Drops	68
雨 Rain	70
霧 Fog	72
湖 A Lake	74
河 A River	76
大海 The Great Sea	78
樹木 Trees	80
草 Grass	82

花 Flowers	84
蜻蜓 A Dragonfly	86
螢火蟲 Fireflies	88
螞蟻 The Ants	90
小雞 Little Chickens	92
公雞 The Cock	94
母雞 The Hen	96
蜘蛛 The Spider	98
蟑螂 Cockroaches	100
壁虎 A gecko	102
房屋 Houses	104
窗 The Window	106
門 The Door	108
桌子 The Desk	110
床 The Bed	112
椅子 The Chair	114
電唱機 The Record Player	116
電視 The Television	118
電話 The Telephone	120

4

蠟燭 The Candle ………… 122
電燈 The Light Bulb ………… 124
燈塔 The Lighthouse ………… 126
氣球 The Balloon ………… 128
飛機 The Airplane ………… 130
風箏 Kites ………… 132
棒球 Baseball ………… 134
足球 Soccer ………… 136
籃球 Basketball ………… 138
洋娃娃 A Doll ………… 140
日本料理店的海 At Sea at a Japanese Restaurant ………… 142
談兒童詩 On Children's Poetry ………… 144
父母捕捉兒童詩語 Some Children's Poetic Language a Father Has Captured ………… 171
兒童文學家傳記 The Brothers Grimm, Two in One ………… 173
作者簡介 An Introduction to Tu Shiu-tien (Sar Po) ………… 186
陳靖奇教授簡介 Translated by Prof. Ching-chi Chen, Ph.d. ………… 192

5

沙白的童詩　黃榮村（考試院院長、前中國醫藥大學校長）

沙白是位專業的牙醫師，但更廣為人知的，他是一位長年勤於筆耕，熱心參與國內外核心詩會活動，在國內外都享有名望的詩人。但更特殊的，也是一般詩人不太敢嘗試的，他一生寫了不少童詩，而且還不是一般應景的童詩都很精簡，但它們大部分都包含有詩歌中的重要元素，如比喻、象徵、與想像力。沙白的童詩都就是說這是給所有人看的詩歌，其中最關鍵的當然就是，孩童們聽了耳朵都會豎起來，而且一聽再聽。

他走入兒童的世界，跟著他/她們思考跟著感覺走，親近兒童喜歡的事物與具有童趣的題材，譬如說：天空、星星月亮太陽、自然界、風水山海、小動物與動物園、玩具與家具、家人、學校等等。這些題目無一不可入詩，無一不是詩。

假如沙白沒有回歸初心，只是當作詩來寫，則很快會在進出之間被敏感敏銳的小孩抓到，因為他很快看出是為賦童詩而強做幼稚之語而已。所以沙白的高明在此，簡單也在此，因為他很快回歸初心融入場景，唯有在此基礎上，與兒童一起呼吸一起共感，用同樣的語言，都是朋友，所以詩行走到後面，若忍不住偶有教化之語，也是自然而然冒出來，孩童也能很快入心。

我們都曾有過童年，大部分的人多以鄉愁與懷念，來回憶觸接自己的童年，我們對童年其實還是很有感覺的，只是有點像隔岸相望，中間有一段很長的心理距離。我們應該有更好的方式可以回去童年，與現在的小孩成為朋友，一起生活在大家有共同感覺，用同樣話的方式成長與學習環境。感謝沙白，他為我們這些寫詩的人，做了一個難得的示範。我們不見得回得去，但是至少我們知道這是可能的，因為沙白經常回去。他用豐富多元又簡短的童詩告訴我們，兒童們其實都在那裡等著我們，要我們有空就一起來玩，一起走入有共同感覺的世界。

6

A Foreword
Sar Po's Children's Poetry

— **Jong-Tsun Huang (黃榮村), former President,
the Examination Yuan, Republic of China;
former Minister of Education, Republic of China;
and former President, the Chinese Medical University at Taichung.**

Sar Po, a well-known dentist and a well-known poet, has been diligently working on the writing of poetry. He has been in good association with other poets in their daily contact and during some important gatherings. Other poets write poetry for the general reading public; yet, in addition to poetry for the general reading public, Sar Po writes children's poetry which is easy to read and is loved by children. In it, he structures his imagination through the eye of children with some rhetoric techniques, such as comparison (metaphor and simile), symbols, etc. His poetry has been enjoyed by adults and children.

In his children's poetry, he leads us, adults and children alike, in the world conceived through the eye of children. In the poetry, objects such as the sky, the sun, the moon, stars, the sea, rivers, and mountains; living things in and out of botanical and / or zoological gardens; toys and furniture; the school and the family, are all his topics.

Let us suppose if Sar Po did not go back to the primordial state of the mind intentionally and wrote his poetry, some sensitive juvenile readers would still be able to locate the existence of the mind in the poetry. The mind is the children's mind. Each and every one of us, adults and children, harbors the children's mind. Sar Po is good at grasping the children's mind in his poetry, so much so that it appeals to adults and children alike. The poetry is enlightening and educating.

Everyone has had his / her childhood and is nostalgic about it. The nostalgia is similar to that of his hometown. There is a long distance between adulthood and childhood; yet, many desire to go back to the latter. There must be a way with which one may go back to it. It seems to me that one may do so in living with children and share with them the nostalgia. I am thankful to Sar Po in giving us the possible way to go back to our childhood, not in the real world but in imagination, in his poetry. Many of his children's poems are concise and full of images conceived through the eye of children. Reading the poems would make it possible for us to be with children and lead us back to our own childhood.

台北市教育局毛連塭局長 序

童詩是兒童心靈自然流露的結晶。

童詩是啟發兒童心靈的最佳鑰匙。

童詩是教育兒童的最佳讀物。

兒童是國家未來的主人翁,教育兒童是大人的天職。大人寫的兒童詩,對兒童詩想的啟迪幫助很大,也可以豐富兒童天真純潔的心靈。

我國是文化大國,自古以來,文學興盛發達,而詩是文學的精華,歷代如金珠玉環的燦爛詩篇,一直滋養著人類的心靈。

童詩乃詩之一環,近年來蓬勃發展。沙白為詩人醫生,醫術精湛,於求學時期即熱愛文學,今於行醫之餘,仍對文學研究和創作不輟,並有傑出之創作,今將其童詩出版,為兒童詩壇綻開鮮麗的奇葩,供給大家欣賞。

前高雄市教育局長
現任台北市教育局長

民國七十五年七月

Foreword

— **By Mao Lianwen, Commissioner, Bureau of Education, Taipei City and formerly Commissioner, Bureau of Education, Kaohsiung City.**

Children's poetry is a crystallization of a spontaneous overflow of the children's emotions.

Children's poetry is the best key to open up the mystery of children's mind.

Children's poetry is the best text for children to read in the education of them.

Children are the future of our nation. To educate them is the duty of us the adults.

The adults write poems for children and, through them, we may enlighten their mind and enrich their innocent imagination.

Our nation is one of rich culture. Since ancient times, the production of literature has been abundant. Poetry is the essence of literature. Verses and poems, which are like gold pearls and jade bracelets brilliant to the eye, nourish the mind of the humankind.

Children's poetry has been flourishing in recent years. Sar Po, a poet and dentist, is excellent in his dentistry and in his love for literature. He was enamored of literature in his younger days. As a practicing dentist, he is still interested in doing research in and writing literature. The outcome of his writing is here for us. This collection of children's poetry is something awesome for us to enjoy.

涂院長秀田 惠鑒：

　　時序季夏荔月之際，蓮渚風清，梅庭月朗，敬維諸事，百務迪吉，維祝維頌！

　　素仰 院長學養卓越，奉獻醫學揚名國際，長年勤於文學創作，成就頗豐，績效斐然，深為各界仰望與敬重，文壇譽為「國際詩人」，曷勝抃賀！

　　欣悉 院長大作「星星愛童詩」、「星星亮晶晶」、「唱歌的河流」三本兒童詩集，與國立高師大前英文所所長暨文學院院長陳靖奇教授合作翻譯成英文，並編印成華英雙語的雋永詩冊，供為兒童雙語文學之優良讀物。

　　今喜見大作付梓在即，耀昌願以歡喜之情樂以為推薦，讓優良文學創作得以向下扎根，以培育更多的後輩文學人才，啟發無窮無盡的創新。

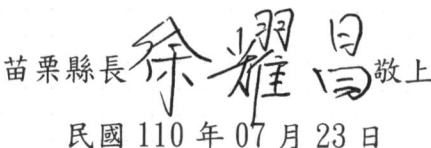

苗栗縣長 徐耀昌 敬上
民國110年07月23日

耀昌用箋

Dear Dr. Shiu-tien Tu:

At the time of mid-summer, when all kinds of fruit are ripe and flowers are blossoming, I wish you well.

Your reputation as a dentist and an international poet is well known to us. It is also known that you are well learned and have written extensively in prose and poetry.

It is a pleasure for us to find that three collections of your children's poetry, Twinkle, Twinkle, Little Stars, Stars Love Children's Poetry and Singing Rivers, will be published with their Chinese and English texts. The English rendition was done by Ching-chi Chen, Ph.d., Professor Emeritus of English, National Kaohsiung Normal University. I believe that our children will benefit from the reading of them.

Knowing that their publication would be good for education of our students / pupils, I strongly recommend them to our teachers and parents.

                    With best regards, I am
                    Sincerely yours,
                    Yao-chang Hsu (徐耀昌),
                    Magistrate, Miaoli County, Taiwan,
                    Republic of China.
                    July 23, 2021.

大家都曾上牙科診所看過牙醫，年幼時也都有讀過童詩。牙醫和詩人是很少有交集的兩種專業。但沙白（涂秀田牙醫師）卻能一手幫病人植牙，另一隻手執筆寫出生動的童詩，長期專注地耕耘，他在杏壇和「詩領域」，都散發出耀人的光芒。

沙白寫詩很早，就讀高雄醫學院時，就擔任阿米巴詩社的社長，也是心臟詩社、布穀鳥詩社的成員；他的詩集「太陽的流聲」、「星星亮晶晶」和「星星愛童詩」等，都曾被譯為日文、韓文，在外國的詩壇被廣為推介。

沙白的詩作受到肯定，他也多次受邀參加亞洲詩人大會、世界詩人大會，和世界華文兒童文學筆會等。

沙白的三本兒童詩集「星星亮晶晶」、「星星愛童詩」、「唱歌的河流」，其內容均經國立高雄師範大學前英語所所長暨文學院院長陳靖奇教授翻譯成英文，可中英對照閱讀，是兒童雙語文學的優良讀物，特此推薦。

南投縣長 林明溱 謹識

Everybody has visited a dentist and read children's poetry, but dentistry and children's mixed together are rarely seen. Sar Po (Dr. Shiu-tien Tu) can treat his patients' teeth with one hand and write children's poetry with the other. Having written prose and poetry for a long time, he is well known to all.

Sar Po began to write poetry at an early age when he was studying at Kaohsiung Medical University. There he was a member of the following clubs of poetry: The Amoeba Club of Poetry (where he used to serve as its President), The Heart Club of Poetry and The Cuckoo Club of Poetry. Some of his poems in the three collections of his children's poetry, Twinkle, Twinkle, Little Stars, Stars Love Children's Poetry and Singing Rivers, were translated into Japanese and Korean. They are welcome overseas.

He received acclaims from everywhere. He was invited to attend The Asian Congress for Poets, The World Congress for Poets, and the World Congress for Children's Literature in Chinese many times.

The three collections of his children's poetry, Twinkle, Twinkle, Little Stars, Stars Love Children's Poetry and Singing Rivers, will be published with their Chinese and English texts. The English rendition was done by Ching-chi Chen, Ph.d., Professor Emeritus of English, formerly Dean of Liberal Arts, National Kaohsiung Normal University. I believe that our children will benefit from the reading of them.

Knowing that their publication would be good for education of our students / pupils, I strongly recommend them to our teachers and parents.

                                            Mingzhen Lin (林明溱)
                                            Magistrate, Nantou County, Taiwan,
                                            Republic of China.

Penghu County Government

澎湖縣政府

涂院長秀田勛鑒

涂院長醫學揚名國際，文學創作豐碩，文壇譽為「國際海洋詩人」。「星星愛童詩」、「星星亮晶晶」、「唱歌的河流」等三本童詩，是我國兒童文學珍貴資產。今與高師大陳靖奇教授合作，將純真雋永的詩篇，編印華、英雙語推廣，令人敬佩。編印之際，謹祝發揚光大，世界看見臺灣兒童文學之美。

祝福您與家人平安健康。

澎湖縣 縣長

   謹上

110 年 5 月 21 日

澎湖縣馬公市治平路32號
32 Chihping RD, Makung Penghu, Taiwan R.O.C
Tel:886-6-9272300 Fax:886-6-9264060

Dear Dr. Shiu-tien Tu,

    Your being an expert in dentistry and having written extensively in prose and poetry have helped establish your reputation as a renowned dentist and an international poet. Your three collections of children's poetry, Twinkle, Twinkle, Little Stars, Stars Love Children's Poetry and Singing Rivers, to be published with their Chinese and English texts can be an asset to our education. The English rendition done by Ching-chi Chen, Ph.d., Professor Emeritus of English, National Kaohsiung Normal University, would help the students to enjoy the beauty of poetry and to learn English for their daily life. I believe that our children will benefit from the reading of them in their enjoyment of Taiwan's children's literature and learning of English.

    With best regards, I remain
Sincerely yours,
Feng-wui Lai (賴峰偉),
Magistrate, Penghu County, Taiwan,
Republic of China.
May 21, 2021.

邁出了第二步
——談沙白的人和詩

沙白是學醫的，但是他更喜歡文學和孩子。就因為這樣，他跟許多兒童文學工作者成了朋友。沙白寫作勤，除了經常為報紙、雜誌撰稿以外，在文學創作方面寫得多的是新詩。他愛上了兒童文學以後，很自然的也為孩子寫了不少的詩。去年，他把他為孩子寫的詩編成一個集子「星星亮晶晶」，這是他向兒童詩邁出的第一步。今年，他又把一年來為孩子寫的詩編成第二個集子「星星愛童詩」。這是他向兒童詩邁出的第二步。

沙白天性爽朗，再加上意識到他的讀者是小孩子，所以他寫的詩都很明朗。例如他寫的「河流」，就有這樣的特色：

　　我是一條喜歡旅行的河流

　　從上游到下游

　　從山上游到海口

　　轉了千個彎

　　唱了萬首歌

　　日日夜夜流

他既然已經喜歡上了兒童詩，自然會繼續走下去，「深入蠻荒」，尋找屬於他自己的綠洲，他很謙虛，承認他為兒童寫的詩是一種嘗試。其實，那就是他對兒童詩的探索。

林良

16

一個寫兒童詩的人，難免接觸到一些「兒童詩論」。沙白曾經談起：這些詩論大大困擾了他。我想，這是他求好心切的緣故。

詩論的作者，在詩論裏表達了他對「詩」的意見。詩論的多樣化，提高了「詩論領域」的價值。閱讀詩論可以增長我們對「詩」的見識。詩論的可讀，就在詩論作者的各說各話。就因為詩論作者的各說各話，才能對我們的創作產生一些刺激作用。如果天下的詩論竟出現空前的一致，甚至出現了範本，那麼一切創作就都將停工。

我們的小學裏，因為有「童詩教學」活動，在教學過程上不能沒有一定的「秩序」，所以無法避免採用比較科學的態度來處理童詩。童詩必須有「定義」，包括它的性質、形式、內容。一首詩的好壞，要有明確的立即判斷的標準。以這樣的立場寫出來的詩論，對創作者來說，讀起來當然更是「怕怕」。

購買的先決條件是必須有我們所要的貨品。如果沒有，就只好先放下購買意願，鼓勵製造。我們的童詩世界，目前最需要的是對創作的鼓勵，而不是對創作的「管理」。創作要有良好的環境。良好的環境不是指一間安靜的房間，而是指一種期待的氣氛。

期待的氣氛是：一個人寫了一千首詩，其中只要有一首是你所喜愛的，就立刻介紹給廣大的讀者欣賞。期待要有恒不變，對作者要愛護。慢慢的，我們也就能有好詩「三百首」了。

期待的氣氛不是：一個人剛開始寫了第一首詩，令你失望，就兇狠狠的把他罵回去。

17

純淨可愛的詩論，其實也並不困擾人；不但不困擾人，反而對創作者有幫助。沙白讀得較多而感到困擾的是可怕的「詩罵」。我很希望擅長寫「詩罵」的人，換一種稿紙，靜下心來依自己的主張多從事創作，多為孩子寫幾首可讀的好詩。

以我國現在兒童詩的總成績來說，自己多種些好花。而且越種越多，總比罵別人小園裏種的都是野草，扛着鋤頭到處巡視，到處剷除好得多。詩的大地是無比的廣濶。

我對沙白說：好詩是歲月和智慧的結晶。對詩，既要朝朝暮暮，也要天長地久。希望我們彼此對對方都有一份期待。你的勤於探索，使我相信你會比我更早找到你自己的綠洲。

（序文作者為中華民國兒童文學會理事長）

七十六年九月五日在台北

Marching out the Second Step:
a Discussion of Sar Po, the Man and His Poetry

──**Foreword by Lin Liang**

Sar Po majored in dentistry, yet he is also interested in children and literature. That is why he has made friends with people working in the field of literature. He has produced a lot of works and had them published in newspapers and magazines. Among the works, poetry, both new and children's, constitutes the majority. Loving children, he wrote poetry for them. The first collection of children's poetry is entitled, Twinkle, Twinkle, Little Stars. Now, the second collection, Stars Love Children's Poetry, is here with us. That is why I call it marching out the second step.

Sar Po is an open-minded person and, knowing that he is writing poetry for children, his poetry is easy to read. He describes the river as follows:

I am a river who likes to travel,
From up-streams to down-streams, and
From the mountains to the sea.
I make hundreds upon hundreds of turns and
Sing thousands upon thousands of songs,
Day and night.

I believe that, loving children's poetry, he would continue to write more. Marching into the wilds, he would find his oasis. He is humble in saying that writing children's poetry is only a new try. In truth, he is exploring a terra incognito.

To write children's poetry, he has read some poetics on it. Oftentimes, he said that poetics on children's poetry had puzzled him. I believe that the puzzlement is a sign of his desiring to write better poetry.

It seems to me that a writer on his own poetics has his own view of poetry writing. Reading poetics on children's poetry would of course enhance our view on it, but different theories on its writing could sometimes be conflicting. Indeed, different views could offer us different ideas on children's poetry. If all views are the same and unified, there would be no need to write more poetry.

In our primary schools, we have the course, Reading of Children's Poetry. There should be a definitive form of the course. We could not avoid applying some scientific approaches toward the teaching. In the teaching of children's poetry, the elements of the course are as follows: its nature, its form and its content. Whether or not a poem is a children's poem, there is a strict definition. Regrettably, poetry that meets the above-mentioned qualities would be something unwelcome to the writers.

In shopping for goods, we purchase the ones that satisfy our demand. If there is none in the market, we may turn to the production of new goods that satisfy our needs. In the same manner, we may write children's poetry that can satisfy our needs in the classroom. At present, what we need should be encouragement to write good children's poetry, not trying to administer its writing according to the rules set by any authority. In short, what we need is a good environment where poetry can be produced.

A good environment is not one that just offers a quiet space, but an atmosphere where we may anticipate something good and suitable for the writing of poetry. In an atmosphere where such anticipation occurs, the poet may compose a thousand pieces of poetry, only one of which may be to the liking of the readers. This only one can be publicized and introduced to the general public. Feeling of anticipation should be there, and the poet should be encouraged. Little by little, poems produced can amount to as many as Three Hundred Poems of the Tang Dynasty.

In an atmosphere where anticipation occurs, a disappointing poem might be produced. We might negatively criticize its inadequacy according to rules we have set.

Frankly speaking, an acceptable poetics is not that horrible and puzzling. It might help the poet along in his writing. I know that many negatively criticize some of the poems by Sar Po. I wish that those who criticize would leave him alone and try to write poems themselves for the good of the children.

It seems to me that in the garden of children's poetry, we should plant more flowers. We should not claim that flowers planted by others might be weeds. We should not carry hoes everywhere trying to destroy flowers planted by others as weeds. The more flowers there are, the better. The Good Earth is immense and is able to contain all.

I would like to say to Sar Po that good poetry is a crystallization of time and wisdom. Poetry is about temporariness and eternity. We should hope him well. We believe that, ceaselessly exploring in the realm of poetry, he would find his oasis.

By Lin Liang, President of the Association of Children's Literature, Republic of China, September 1987.

童心童趣的再現

——序詩人沙白的童詩集「星星亮晶晶」

我的朋友韓國兒童文學家宣勇先生，他曾經用標準的中國話對我說過：「童心是成人心裡的故鄉。」這是一九八二年三月二十一日他來台北訪問時，我們在閒談中談到的有關從事兒童文學寫作的一句話，四年多了，他這句話，一直縈繞在我的腦海裡，只要我一想到為兒童寫作的事情，它就會浮現出來，導引着我去思考有關的問題。

現在，詩人沙白先生要出版他的第一本童詩集，把他近兩年來所寫而都已發表了的童詩寄給我，要我給他寫一篇序，我細細的拜讀之後，發覺到：他的童詩，彷彿也就是宣勇先生所說的，表達了一個成人從現實世界裡，尋找到自己「心裡的故鄉」我為他感到無限欣喜和慰藉。

為兒童寫詩，童心、童趣的掌握與再現，是和詩質的把握同其重要。有了童心，自然會事事以兒童「純真」的觀點來看世界，有了童趣，自然會掌握到兒童的心理，為他們呈現足以

22

令人會心一笑而又有所感觸的滋潤心靈的意味，加上詩人本身長時對詩學修鍊的工夫而充分掌握詩質，就容易完成一篇篇優異的童詩作品。

個人一直以為：成人為兒童寫詩，是一種愛的表現，我們有責任用最好的語言，最愉快的心境，最純真的意念，最真摯的感情，最靈活的想像，最新的思想……來為他們寫詩。拜讀詩人沙白的這本童詩集，我們也可以肯定能從中獲得這樣的精神和保證，因為他已經朝着一條可喜的方向邁進，使我們欣賞他的詩，也能分享到他寫作時充滿着喜悅的那份心境，純真可愛。

詩人、兒童文學家
現任：中華民國兒童文學會總幹事
七十五年七月二十六日上午在東湖

Representation of the Children's Mind and Interest

— Lin Huanzhang, a writer in children's poetry and Director General, the Republic of China Association for Children's Literature, July 26, 1986, at Donghu.

My friend, a Korean writer in children's literature, said to me in standard Mandarin, "The mind of children is the homeland of the mind of adults." The remark was made on March 21, 1982, when he visited Taipei. At that time, we discussed things concerning the writing of children's literature. That was four years ago. Since then, the idea has kept popping up in my mind regarding the writing of children's literature. I have been reconsidering the remark.

Sar Po, the poet, said to me that he wanted to have his first collection of children's poetry published and asked me to write a foreword. After I have read his manuscript, the idea proposed by my Korean friend, can be found there in the poetry. I am immensely pleased and satisfied with the poetry in that the adult poet who deals with the realities in writing children's poetry have found "the homeland of the mind of adults."

To be able to grasp children's mind and interest in the writing of children's poetry is as important as being able to deal with the quality of poetry. With children's mind, the poet is able to see the world in children's innocent view; with children's interest, he is able to grasp children's psychology and to touch our heart. The reader will be able to participate in the joy. With the best quality of poetry, the poet is able to produce the best children's poetry.

It seems to me that an adult who writes children's poetry should be equipped with love for children. He should employ the best language, the happiest mood, the purest will, the sincerest emotions, the most lively imagination and the newest thinking. Reading Sar Po's poems in this collection, I can read such elements as mentioned above. I promise that he has marched out on the path where one can enjoy the pleasure, innocence and excitement he has put in his writing of children's poetry.

自序

以童心寫的詩叫做童詩。

童詩是人籟之最天真和最美妙的聲音。

童詩是人類心靈的搖籃。

我們寫詩就像花木綻放美麗的花朵，除了顯示自我美麗的存在之外，還給別人欣賞漂亮的容姿。燦爛奪目的花之麗質，除了決定於她的遺傳之外，後天的培養也很重要。一隻狗永遠不會成為一隻老虎，但是，一隻會演戲的老虎是靠訓練得來的。同理，沒有詩胚子的人，很難寫出好詩。寫好詩除了需要有詩胚子之外，後天的培養也很重要，詩仙李白，天才稟異，詩聖杜甫，詩風雄渾，他們如果不努力讀書的話，也寫不出永垂不朽的詩篇。諾貝爾獎詩人T·S·艾略特，更是學富五車，他精研古今文學、宗教、哲學等，因此，他的詩想深厚龐沛，寫詩能夠引用許多典故，論詩也能夠旁徵博引而理析出一套精奧微妙的理論。

小孩寫童詩，也須先讀書，才能夠啟發詩想和運用詩的語言。成人寫童詩，除了讀書之外，小孩回輸給成人的詩想也很重要，譬如，我三個小孩就成為我的活生生的教本給了我許多

沙白

寫童詩的靈感。

我覺得兒童詩有許多效用，如：

①使兒童認識更多的文字，並活用更多的文字，使之生命化和鮮活化。

②培養兒童天真的童心，使之更純潔可愛。

③啟發兒童的想像力，使他對自己及家庭、社會和四周的萬物更關心，而溶入其中，並創造詩的新世界。

④培育兒童更深厚的同情心，薰陶兒童美育和德育的心靈，增加生活的趣味和快樂。

⑤增進兒童的知識，成為社會的好人。

⑥引發和培養兒童對文藝的興趣。

⑦引導兒童的心理情緒走向正常的軌道。

⑧兒童寫童詩，可以在潛意識及意識裡，確立其存在之意義和價值，並展現其人生的理想。

因此，兒童詩的創作及教育是我國教育裡極重要的一環，我希望本詩集，能夠像一棵花，長在兒童文學園地裡，引起大家欣賞的樂趣。

Preface

—Sar Po.

Children's poetry is written with children's mind.

Children's poetry is an echo in the human world of its beautiful sounds.

Children's poetry is the cradle of the human mind.

The writing of children's poetry is like the blooming of flowers. Their beauty could be in itself and might move their viewers. The quality of beautiful flowers is determined by not only their genes but also their cultivation. Truly, a dog can never be a tiger; yet, a tiger can be trained to act in a circus. In the same manner, a person without an aptitude for poetry is not able to write good poetry. To write good poetry, he has not only to have the aptitude but also to be able to practice writing it. The Tang poets, such as Li Po and Du Fu who can be models of having the aptitude and being able to write poems out of their experiences, were highly gifted and majestic in their poetic contents and styles. Furthermore, the Nobel laureate, T. S. Eliot was well learned. He was well versed in classic and modern literature, religions, philosophy, etc. His poetry is profound in thoughts and meaning. In many of his poems, allusions to previous works by other writers can be found, and the same can be true of his other works such as plays and prose. From his reading of world classics and history, he could work out his own ideas of life and literature.

A child intending to write children's poetry has also to study. In his studies, he can find words and ideas fit for poetry. In addition to studying, an adult poet has to go back to his childhood to look for the long lost experiences. I have found the inspiration for poetry from the experiences of my three children.

The advantages of children's poetry reading can be as follows:

- It helps children get acquainted with words and use them in their daily life.
- It helps children keep their innocent mind and make them purer and more lovable.
- It helps enliven children's imagination and cultivate their love for their family, society and things around them in a newfound world.
- It helps children be sympathetic and empathetic with others and be good citizens in the future.
- It helps children gain knowledge and educate them in aesthetics and morals in order that they may live a happier and more interesting life.
- It helps children be interested in arts and literature.
- It helps children stabilize their emotions and put them back to a normal track of life.
- Children who write poems would consciously and unconsciously get acquainted with the meaning of existence and form their own ideals for the coming life.

Therefore, it seems to me that reading of children's poetry and its education would be important in our primary-school curriculum.

I wish that the collection would be like a flower in the garden of children's literature leading everyone to the interest of reading.

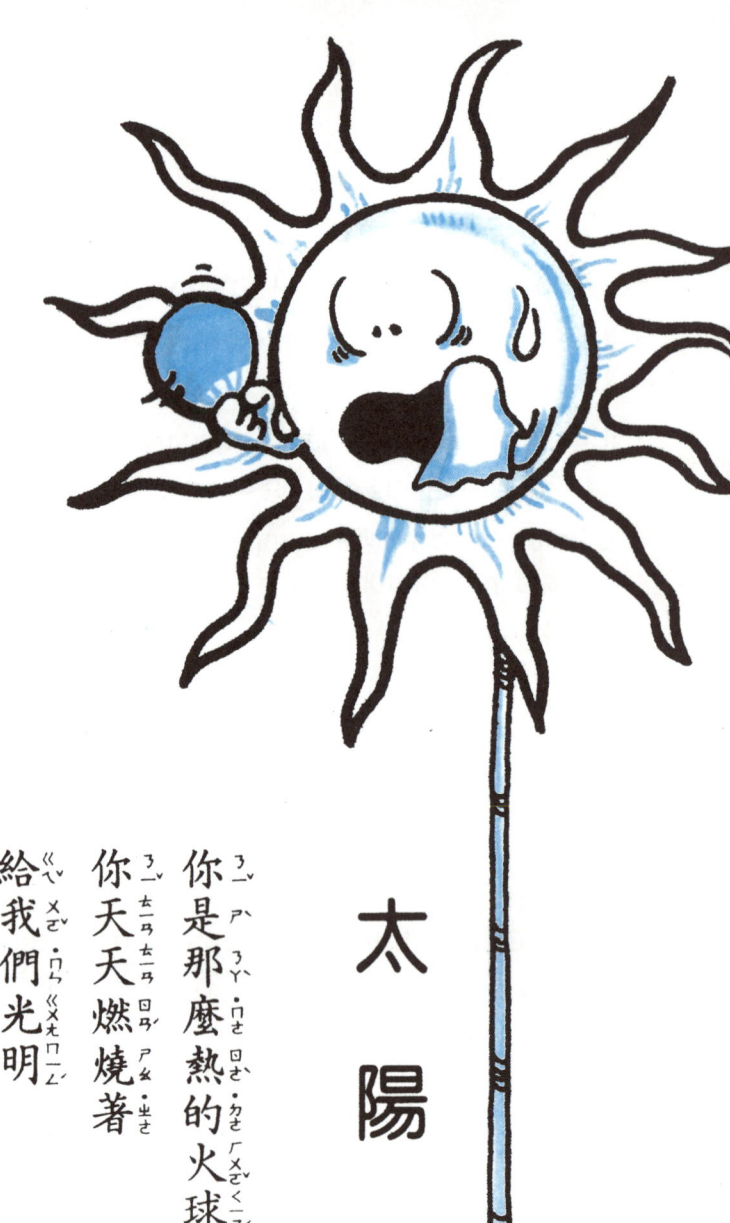

太陽

你是那麼熱的火球
你天天燃燒著
給我們光明
你是免費的電燈泡
你是巨大的電燈泡
多麼明亮的燈泡喲
你別燒壞了

The Sun

You are a fiery ball,
Burning every day.
You give us light.
You are a light bulb free of charge.
You are a huge light bulb.
How bright you are!
Please don't burn yourself.

月亮

妳高掛在天空上
是誰把妳掛上去的
是太空戰士嗎
是嫦娥姐姐嗎
天上不是很冷嗎
請下來跟我們玩吧

The Moon

You hang up high in the sky.
Who put you up there?
Is it a space fighter who did this?
Or, is it Sister Chang-o?
Isn't it cold high up there?
Would you please come down to play with us?

小星星

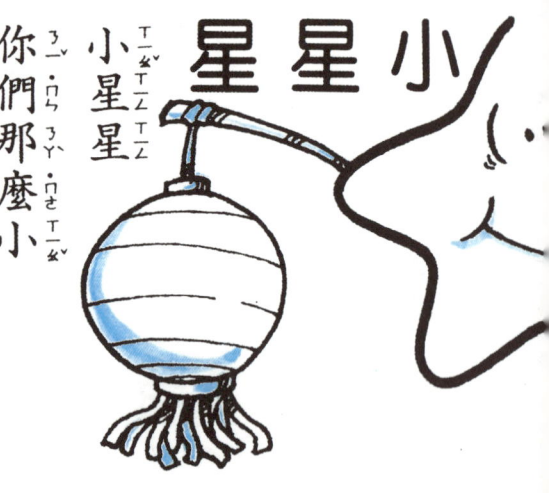

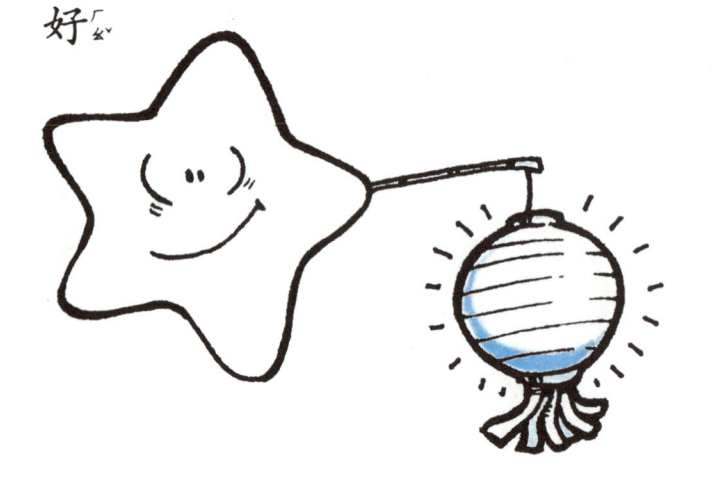

小星星
你們那麼小
像一群螢火蟲
你們的兄弟姐妹那麼多
好可愛
為什麼站得那麼高
你們不怕烏雲吃掉嗎
快快下來跟我們玩
我們有很多朋友要跟你們好

Little Stars

Little stars,
How small you are!
You are like fireflies.
You have many brothers and sisters.
You are lovely.
Why do you stand up high in the sky? 
Aren't you afraid of being devoured by the black clouds?
Come down to play with us quickly.
Many of us want to make friends with you.

春風

春風吹來眞清爽
好像母親給我搖紙扇
母親說春風吹一陣
小孩就會長三寸
我願多吹春風
多長十寸

Spring Breezes

Spring breezes blow to me.
I feel refreshed as if my mother was shaking a paper fan.
My mother says that when spring breezes blow
Children would grow three inches taller.
I wish that spring breezes would blow more
So that I would grow ten inches taller.

海風

海風向漁夫說
太陽那麼熱
打魚那麼辛苦
我吹一陣涼爽的風
給你們當汽水喝
喝得舒舒服服

Sea Breezes

Sea breezes asked fishermen:
"The sun is so sultry,
Why do you take the trouble of going fishing?
We shall blow to you
And make you feel cool as having drunk cool soda.
Then, you will feel comfortable."

颱風

天上沒有掛巨大的電風扇
為什麼風吹得那麼大
你沒有嘴巴
你沒有翅膀
為什麼可以飛得那麼快？
吹得那麼響？

A Typhoon

There is not a huge electric fan in the sky.
How can wind blow so strongly?
You have no mouth,
Nor have you wings.
How can you fly so fast
And blow so loudly?

雪

雪飄落在高高的玉山上
給漂亮的山頂戴上白帽子
你好小氣唷
為什麼不在我家的屋頂戴上白帽子

Snow

Snow falls on high Mount Jade.
You have put a white hat on the mountain top.
You are stingy
Not to have put such a white hat on the roof of my house.

瀑布

遠遠的山上有一匹瀑布
像一塊長長的毛巾
那是給山洗澡用的

Waterfalls

Waterfalls hang down the faraway mountain
Like a long towel.
It seems that it is used to wash its body.

雨

媽媽說:「雨落著像小妹妹流眼淚」。

小妹妹為什麼流淚?

因為想吃糖菓。

爸爸說:「雨為什麼落著?因為它要給口渴的花草喝水」。

嘻!嘻!

小妹妹聽了就害羞了。

Rain

My mother said:
> "Raindrops were like tears of your little sister."

Why did my sister cry?
Because she wanted to have some candies.
My father said, "Why did rain drop?
Because it wanted to quench the thirst of
  grass and flowers."
Hee, hee!
Having heard my parents' comments,
  my sister felt ashamed.

雲

你沒有翅膀為什麼會飛?
你沒有腳為什麼會走?
你跑得那麼快
你飛得那麼急
原來是跟月亮捉迷藏
跟星星做遊戲

The Clouds

You don't have wings, how can you fly?
You don't have feet, how can you walk?
You run very fast,
And you run hurriedly.
Oh, you are playing hide-and-seek with the moon
And you are also playing with the stars.

閃電

在天空上
閃電一亮
像一隻巨大的螢火蟲閃耀
立刻就飛逝了

Lightning

In the sky,
A lightning flashes,
Like a huge firefly shining,
And then disappears.

雷公在天上打起鼓來

轟隆轟隆地響

他不是在演戲

而是教人不要做壞事

雷

Thunder

Father Thunder is beating a drum
Boom, boom.
He is not playing-acting.
He is teaching us not to do bad things.

春天

穿著繁花綠葉的衣服
唱著美妙悅耳的歌
在舒適的天空中行走

Spring

You are wearing clothes in multicolored flowers and
    green leaves.
You are singing songs pleasing to our ear
And loitering comfortably high in the sky.

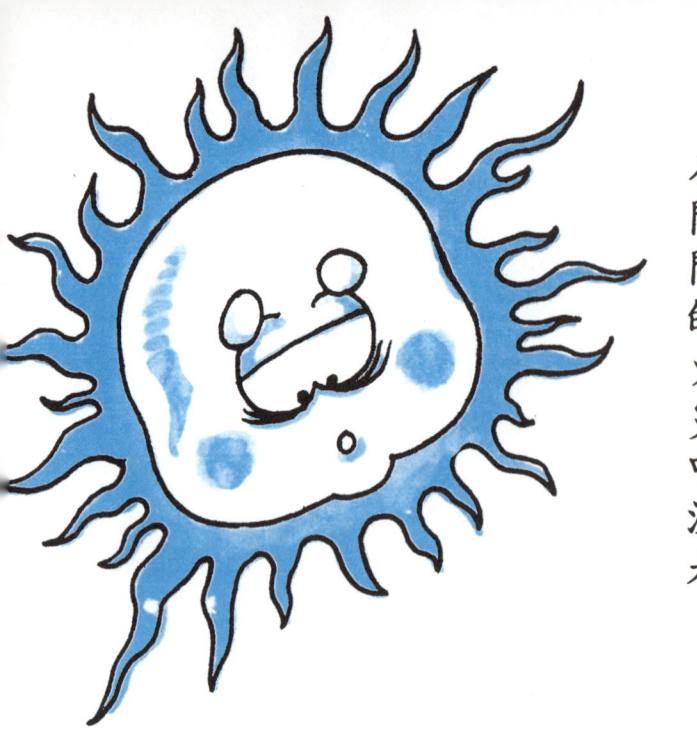

夏天

穿着纍纍果實的綠葉衣服
有熱火爐的輪子
在悶悶的火災中滾走

Summer

You are dressed up in green leaves and plenty of fruits.
With a furnace-like wheel,
The sun is rolling through a stuffy fire.

秋天

穿着破爛的黃葉衣服
在蕭瑟的風中
搖搖欲墜

Autumn

Being dressed in tattered, yellow-leaved clothes,
In chilly wind,
You are walking in a shaky manner.

冬天

有的穿淺綠的衣服
有的衣服被脫得光光
有的衣服將被脫光
有的穿著冷冷的冰雪白衣
在冷風中
凍僵直立

Winter

Some are clothed in light green,
Some are going to be stripped naked,
Some have been stripped naked, and
Others are clothed in cold, white snow.
All are frozen, standing in cold wind.

白天

太陽的眼睛一瞪
懶睡的大地都醒了

Daytime

The sun having opened its eyes
Wakes up the sleepy earth.

黃昏

太陽要下山休息時
喜歡在西天佈置美景
演一場精彩的啞劇
徐徐閉幕

Dusk

Before the sun goes down to take a rest,
He likes to paint a beautiful picture in the western sky.
He is playing a colorful pantomime
To close the day.

黑夜

黑夜像一塊巨大的黑布
蓋着整個大地
我們像捉迷藏
走來走去

Black Night

Black night is like a gigantic black cloth
Covering the earth
Where we run to and fro
To play the game of hide-and-seek.

露

露珠像情人的眼淚
向星星月亮
哭訴了一夜
等待太陽熱情的手
給她擦乾

Dew Drops

Dew drops are like tears from a beloved.
She has been crying
To the moon and stars for a night and
Waiting for the warm hand of the sun
To wipe off her tears.

雨

毛毛細雨像貓叫聲
傾盆大雨像狗吠聲
而我爸爸的笑容
像紅臉溫暖的太陽公公
趕走了惱人的雨聲

Rain

Drizzling is like meowing of cats.
Down-pouring is like barking of dogs.
My father's smiles,
Like the red, warm face of Grandpa Sun,
Will drive away troublesome sounds of raindrops.

霧

整個大地都在抽烟
樹木、房屋、河流都在抽烟
它們抽的是水烟
都趁着太陽公公睡覺時
偷偷地抽
當太陽公公起床後
它們就不敢抽了

Fog

It seems that the whole earth is smoking.
Trees, rivers and houses are all smoking.
They are all smoking hookah.
They are all stealthily smoking
When Grandpa Sun is sleeping.
When Grandpa Sun wakes up,
They will stop smoking.

湖

湖像靜靜安睡的嬰兒
在山林裡
做着新奇綠色的美夢

A Lake

The lake is sleeping quietly
In the forest
Having a strange, green, beautiful dream.

河

河流只有一條腸子
婉婉蠕動着
她吃得不多
永遠是苗條細長的

A River

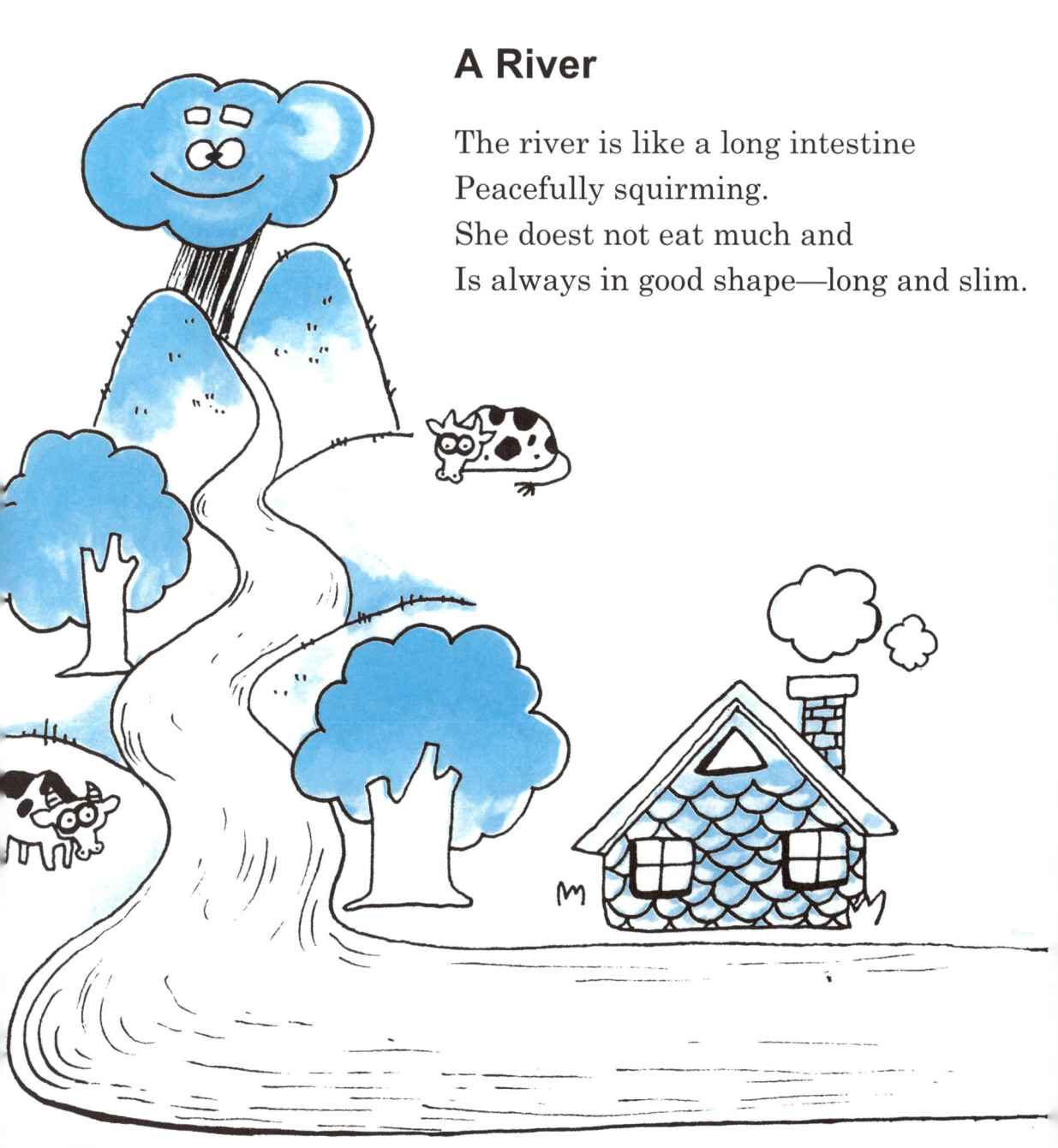

The river is like a long intestine
Peacefully squirming.
She doest not eat much and
Is always in good shape—long and slim.

大海

大海喲
你為什麼那麼大
原來你喝掉全部河流的水
收容了那麼多的雨
吃下那麼多的魚

The Great Sea

The great sea,
Why are you so huge?
Oh, you have drunk all the water from the rivers
And taken all the rain.
You have also eaten so many fish.

樹木

樹枝像長長的手臂
迎接太陽
樹葉像彎彎的雨傘
給我們乘涼
樹木像萬能的機器人
造福世人

Trees

Big trees are like long arms
Reaching out to welcome the sun.
Their leaves are like crooked umbrellas
Giving shades to cool us down.
Trees are also like omnipotent robots
Bringing happiness to us.

草

遍山綠野都是草
你們不吃肥料
也長得那麼好
假如你們可以變為有用的禾苗
我們不愁溫飽

Grass

Everywhere on the meadow on the
　　mountainside, there is grass.
You don't need fertilizer, and
You still grow so well.
If you could become rice paddies,
We would not be starved.

花

各種漂亮的花朵
像世界各國的漂亮小姐
有胖有瘦、有高有矮
穿著美麗的衣服
做時裝表演
不管晴天或下雨
她們都站在花園裡
爭奇鬥艷

Flowers

There are all kinds of flowers.
They are like young, beautiful ladies from different countries.
Some are plump, and others are slim.
Some are tall, and others are short.
They wear beautiful clothes
As in a fashion show.
Rain or shine, they stand in a flower garden,
Contending for their beauty.

蜻 蜓

你是一隻漂亮的小飛機
在河邊草上飛來飛去

你跟我們捉迷藏
哈！哈！好有趣
請問你為什麼不必加汽油
也能飛得那麼久？

A Dragonfly

You are a pretty little airplane,
Flying over the meadow on the riverside.
You are playing hide-and-seek with us.
Ha, Ha, How intesting it is!
May we ask why you can fly so long
Without having to add any gasoline?

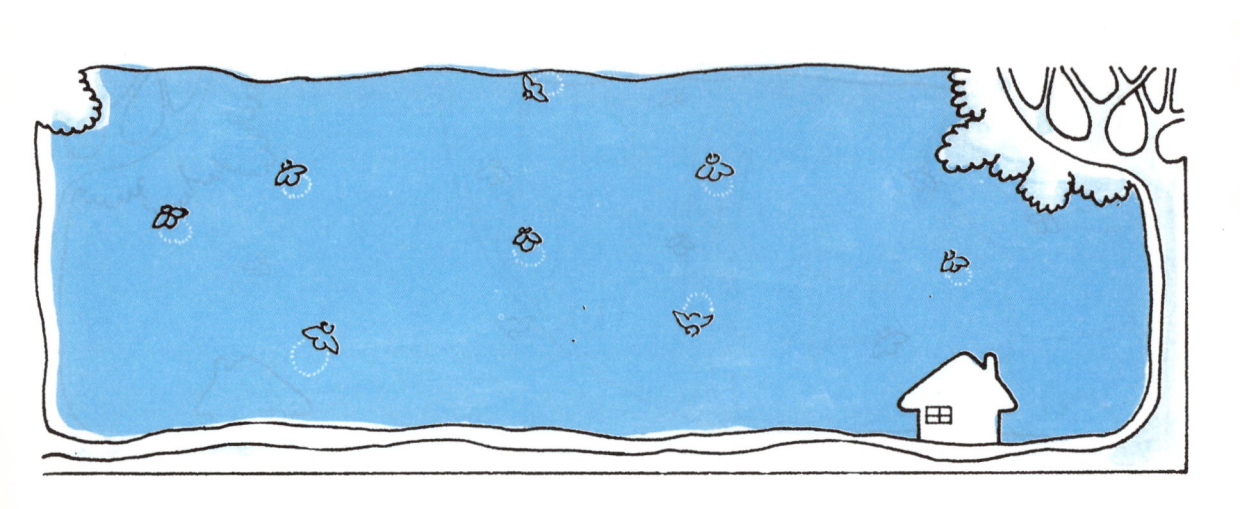

螢火蟲

你在夜之海裡游泳

黑夜的田園像黑色的海洋

那明麗閃閃的游泳旋律

好像發光的小魚在海裡游泳

你像一個善良的聖誕老人

在黑暗中點火引導我們旅行

Fireflies

You seem to be swimming in the nightly sea.
The nightly fields are like a black ocean.
You seem to be swimming in blinkering and twinkling rhythms.
You seem to be swimming like bright little fish in the sea.
You are also like good Santa Claus
Who brings light to illuminate our journey in the dark.

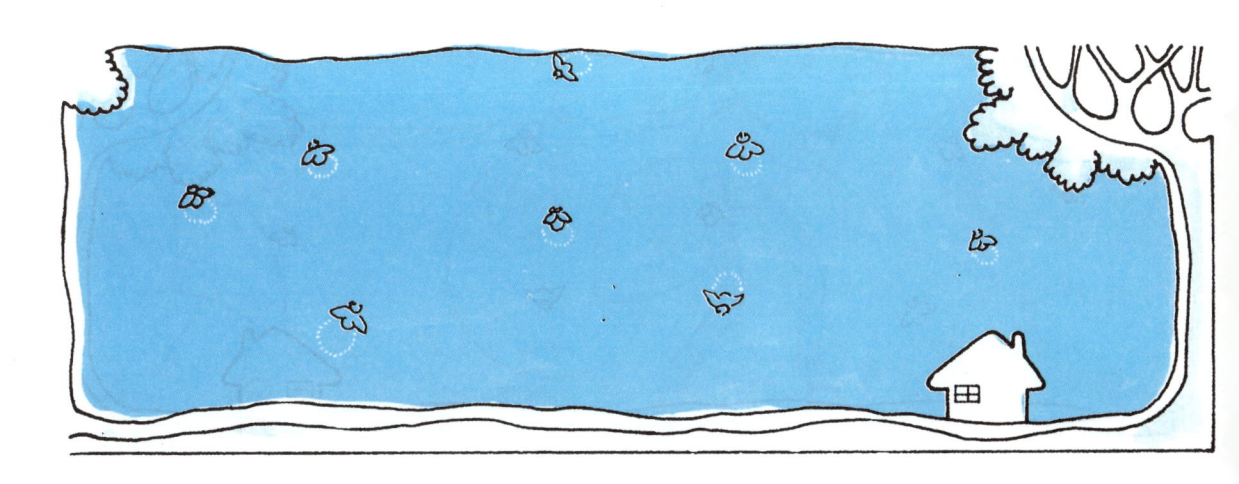

螞蟻

你們成群結隊而行
好像一群工人去築萬里長城
你們勤勞地工作
只建築了小小的泥土房屋
因為你們是會咬人的害蟲
我不蓋房子給你們住
假如你們變為可愛的小蠶
我的房子就給你們住

The Ants

You parade in files
As if workers in groups were going to build a Great Wall.
You work diligently
Only to build a little dirt house.
I would not build one for you
Because you are vermin that bite.
If you were little, lovely silkworms,
I would build one for you.

小雞

小雞們吱吱叫著、玩著

好像小朋友們跳著、玩著

小雞沒有我們快樂

因為我們還會溜滑梯、玩皮球

Little Chickens

Little chickens, you are playing and squeaking
Like small children jumping and playing.
Little chickens, you are not so happy as we are
Because we can slide and play balls.

公雞

母親還沒起床
公雞就起床了
牠不但叫母親起來煮飯
也叫太陽起來發光

The Cock

Before my mother gets out of the bed,
The cock has already woken up.
It wakes up not only my mother to cook breakfast
But also the sun to give light.

母 雞

母雞帶小雞

好像老師帶學生

咯！咯！咯！——

母親啄食物給小雞吃

ㄅㄆㄇㄈ——

老師教學生唸書

The Hen

The hen leads little chickens
As a teacher does her students.
Coo, coo, coo,
The hen is picking up food for the little chickens to eat.
A,B,C,D,
The teacher is teaching her students to read.

蜘蛛

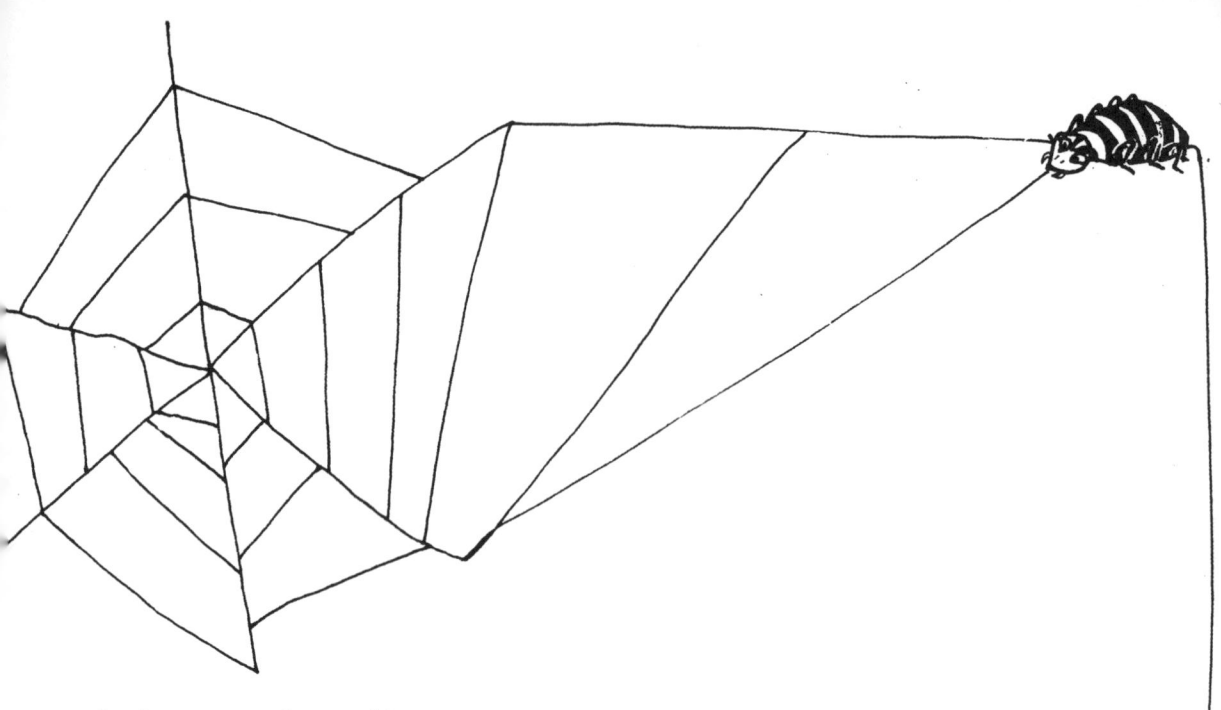

你織成一圈圈的網
像漁夫打魚的網
你的網是狡猾的陷阱
用來捕捉可憐的小蟲

你是不工作的懶惰蟲
每天只等待小蟲投入網中
當做你一個人吃的食物
而勤勞的可愛漁夫
却用魚網打魚給我們大家吃

The Spider

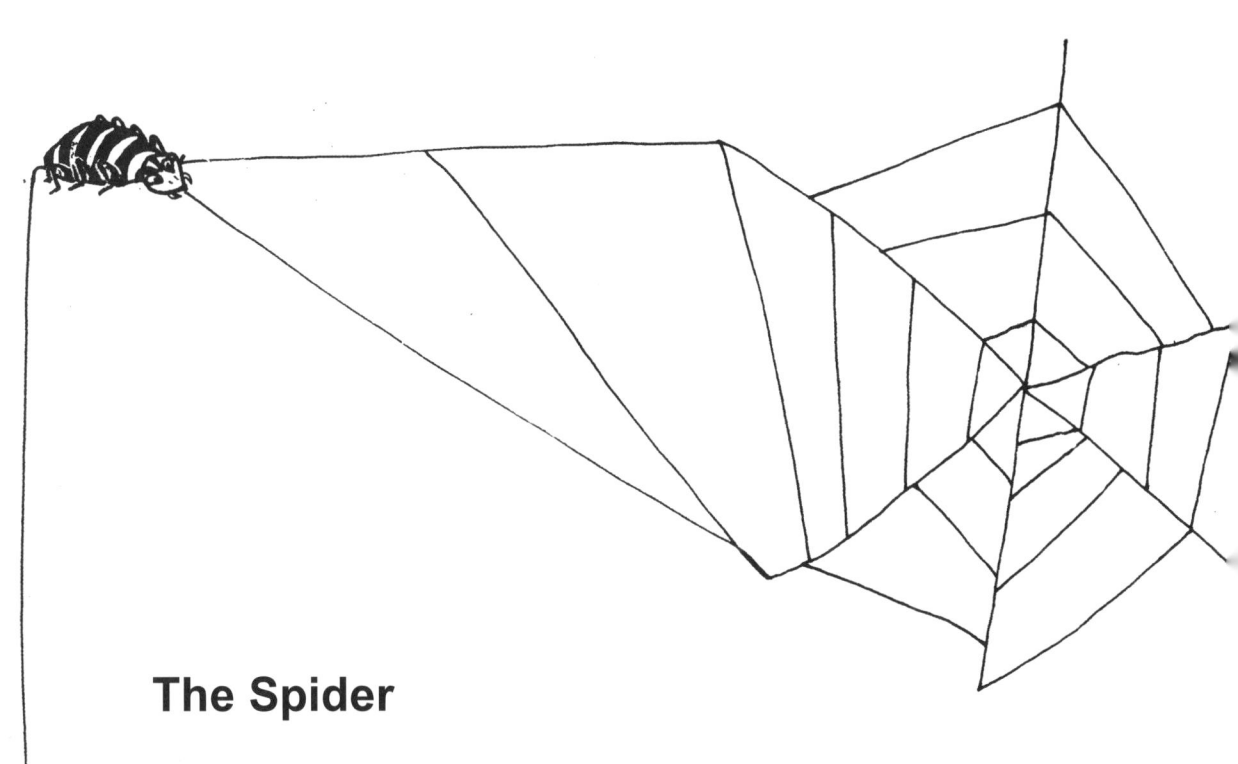

You are weaving a circular web
Like a fishnet that a fisherman would use to catch fish.
Your web is a cunning trap
That would be used to catch poor, small bugs and worms.

You are a lazy vermin
Waiting for bugs and worms to be trapped in your web
For your food.
On the other hand, the fisherman is diligent and lovable
Because he catches fish with his fishnet for us to eat.

蟑螂

你是廚房的小偷
爬來爬去
你有翅膀
為什麼不飛到樹上去
你有長足
為什麼不爬到山上去
你是可惡的臭小偷
我要把你打死

Cockroaches

You are kitchen thieves,
Crawling around.
You got wings.
Why don't you fly up to the trees?
You got feet.
Why don't you climb up to the mountain top?

You are stinking, hateful thieves.
I shall kill you.

壁虎

白色的牆壁那麼滑
而你可以自由自在的爬
你為什麼不變為巨大的老虎
把爬窗的小偷咬死

A gecko

The white wall is so slippery,
How can you climb it up and down freely?
Why can you not be a huge tiger
To scare away thieves who break windows?

房屋

每個房屋像個大鳥籠
總是忙忙碌碌
每天我們進去又出來
出來又進去

我們有了皺紋
它就龜裂成痕

我們老了
它就舊了
原來它的生命和我們一樣
老了以後
也會死亡

Houses

Houses are like big bird cages.
Every day, we go in and out of them;
Every day, we go out of and in them.
We are always going in and out.
As time goes on, we get wrinkles, and
They get cracks.

We grow old, and
They become rickety.

They are like us:
When old,
They will also die.

窗

窗戶是明亮的眼睛
它可以看見室內的東西
和室外的星星
我們要像天天洗臉一樣
把它擦得亮晶晶

The Window

A window is like a bright eye.
Through it, we can see things indoors
And stars outdoors.
Every day, we have to clean it
As we will wash our faces.

門

門是房屋的嘴巴
有時會開一開
像吃東西一樣

The Door

The door is the mouth of the house.
It opens and closes,
As we take in food when we eat.

桌

桌子最用功
一直陪着我讀書
當我外出遊戲時
它還陪着我的書包
默默苦讀

The Desk

The desk is industrious
Accompanying me in my studies all the time.
When I go away from it to play outdoors,
It is still with my book bags,
Silently studying.

床

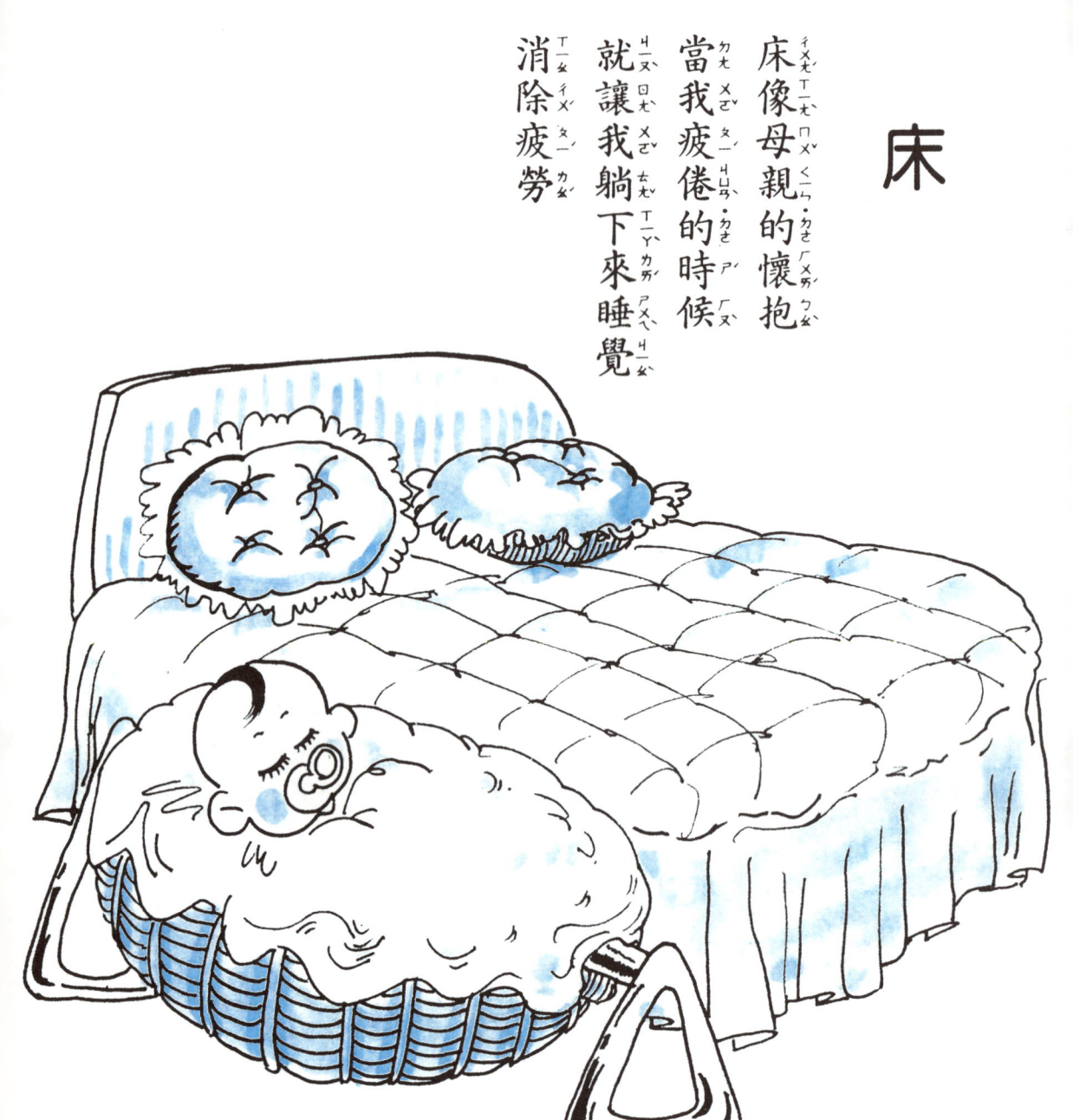

床像母親的懷抱
當我疲倦的時候
就讓我躺下來睡覺
消除疲勞

The Bed

The bed, like my mother's arms,
Holds me while I am tired and
Allows me to lie down to sleep
To get away from fatigue.

椅

椅子像牛背

給我們坐

它從來不發脾氣

比牛還任勞堅毅

The Chair

The chair is like the back of a cow
Allowing me to sit down on it.
The chair never loses its temper.
The chair is more hard working than a cow.

電唱機

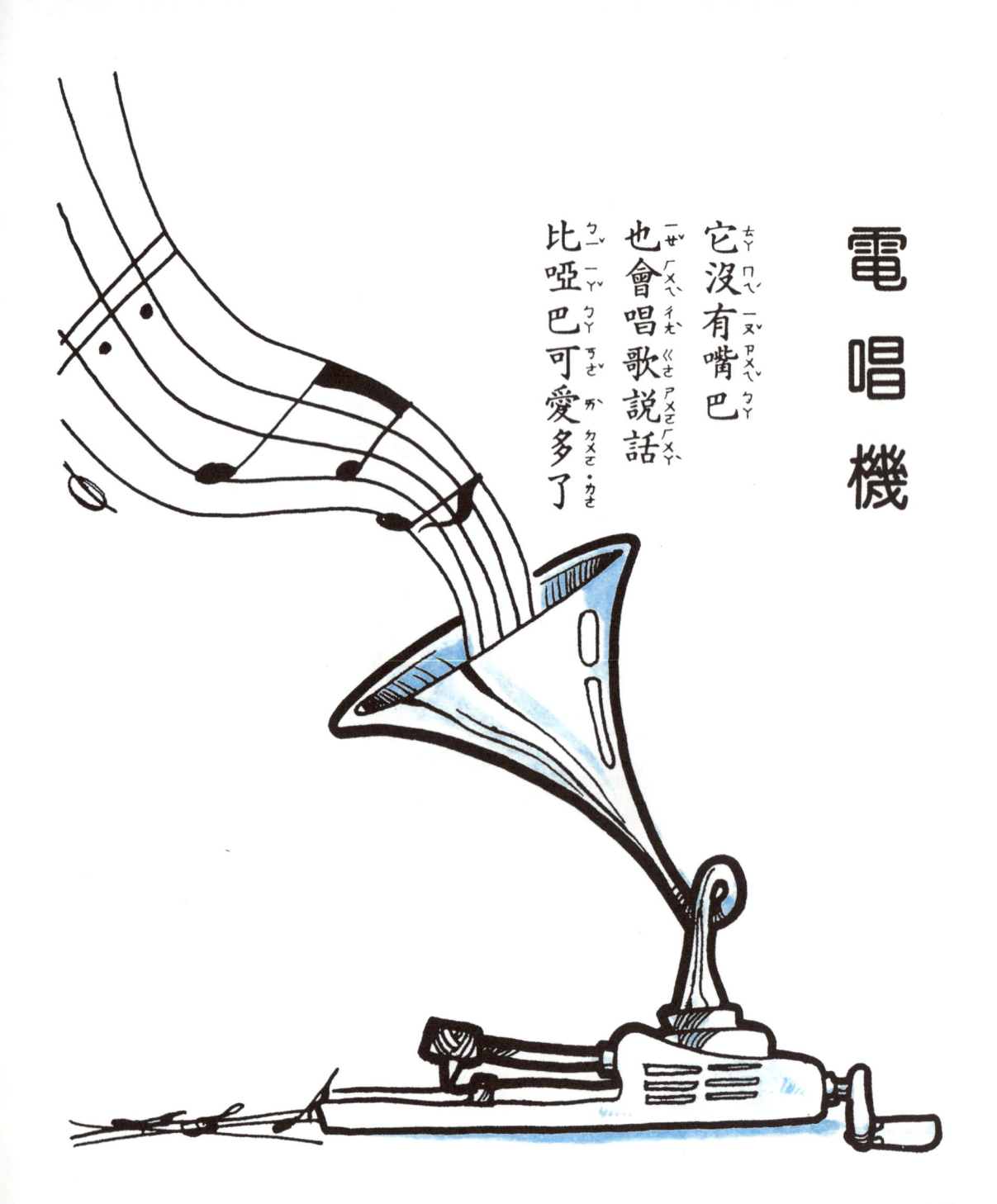

它沒有嘴巴
也會唱歌說話
比啞巴可愛多了

The Record Player

The record player has no mouth,
Yet it can talk and sing songs.
It seems to be more lovable than a mute person.

家家戶戶
有了電視
家家戶戶
都成為小小的電影院

電視

The Television

In every household,
There is a television.
With it, every household
Becomes a movie house.

電話

電話是最快速的電動郵差
只要噥噥一響
就會把我的話
傳給爸爸媽媽

The Telephone

The telephone is a fast electric postman.
As soon as it rings,
It would carry my message
To my father and mother

燭蠟

你為什麼一點火就流淚？
是不是你的光太小，
而黑暗太強？

請別自卑——
小小的針頭，
可以麻醉獅子；
小小的子彈，
可以殺死大象；
星星之火，
可以燎原。

The Candle

Why do you shed tears as soon as you are lighted.
Is it because your light is too dim
To outshine the darkness out there?

Don't be ashamed of yourself.
A little pinpoint of anesthesia would paralyze a lion.
A little bullet would kill an elephant.
A spark of fire
Would burn the whole grassland.

電燈

我們睡覺時
它就關著
像閉口休息一樣
電燈是黑夜的眼睛
它可以看見黑夜裡的東西

The Light Bulb

When we are sleeping,
It is off.
It shuts up and takes a rest.
The light bulb is like an eye in the dark night
Allowing us to see things there.

燈 塔

他高高地站在山上
以燈光的巨手
招呼輪船進港
像慈母的手
呼喚遠方的遊子回鄉

126

The Lighthouse

The lighthouse stands high on the mountain top.
It waves its huge arms of light
To show ships the way to enter the harbor.
Its arms are like those of a mother
Calling her wandering children to come home.

氣球

美麗的氣球飛呀飛的
你們要飛到山上去嗎?
還是飛到海上去?
別飛到那麼遠呀!
會迷路的
請飛來我家好嗎?
我會跟你們做朋友

The Balloon

A beautiful balloon is flying.
Are you flying to the mountain top?
Or, are you flying to the sea?
Please don't fly far away;
Or you will get lost.
Please fly to my home, OK?
I can be friends with you.

飛機

飛機的肚子那麼大
吞食了那麼多旅客
飛到美國
又吐了出去

The Airplane

You got so huge a belly
That you can take in so many passengers.
As soon as you arrive in America,
You will have them out.

風箏

風姐姐吹一吹
我們就飄呀飄的
我們飄得好過癮
我們飄得高高的
要告訴太陽伯伯
我們是多麼地高興

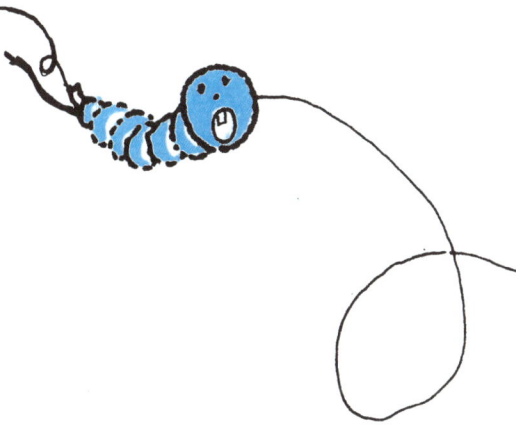

Kites

Sister Wind blows, and
We will fly and float.
We will be enjoying the flight.
We fly and float on high, and
We will tell Grandpa Sun that
We are very happy.

棒球

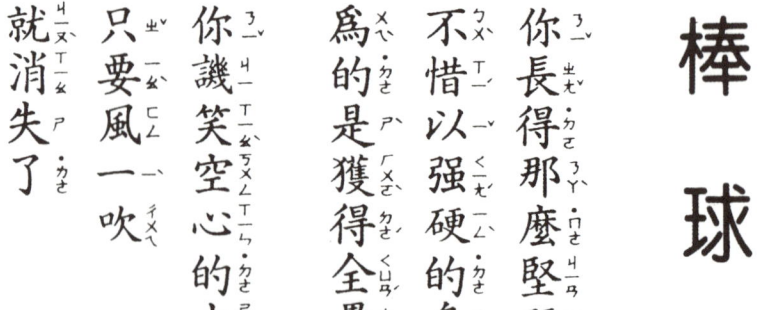

你長得那麼堅硬結實
不惜以強硬的身體碰撞球棒
為的是獲得全壘打的喝采
你譏笑空心的水泡
只要風一吹
就消失了

Baseball

You are so solid that
You are not afraid to touch a club with your strong body
In order that you may hit a home run to win applause from
 the audience.

On the other hand, you laugh at a water bubble which
Would be blown away
By a strong wind.

足球

足球說——
我是被丟在球場的
而你們討厭我
看到我就踢得遠遠的
非得把我踢進門不可

足球想——
原來我長得沒有氣球漂亮
——不能逍遙天空，得意揚揚

Soccer

A soccer says—
I have been kicked around in the field.
It is because you so hate me that
As soon as you see me you would kick me far away.
You are determined to kick me through the gate.

The soccer thinks—
I do not look as beautiful as a balloon,
And I cannot be like it in flying high in the sky triumphantly.

籃球

一個籃球三百元
一張門票一百元
兩隊人馬搶來搶去
兩派觀眾吵來吵去
籃球都不屬於他們的
籃球也不屬於他們的
籃球像小孩被人抱來抱去
最後不屬於任何人的
只屬於他自己

Basketball

A basketball costs three hundred dollars.
An admission ticket costs one hundred dollars.
Two teams are competing for the basketball
Which doesn't belong to either of them.
Two different sides of the audience are arguing over the
 game.
The basketball doesn't belong to them, either.
The basketball, like a child, was being tossed around,
But it doesn't belong to anybody.
It belongs to itself.

洋娃娃

好漂亮的洋娃娃
她凍結在歡樂的兒童夢幻裏
她穿着鵝絨的艷裝
穿着夢的衣裳
日夜做著小天使的時裝表演
給我們欣賞

A Doll

How beautiful the doll is!
She is frozen in children's happy dreams.
She is wearing gorgeous apparel of goose down,
Apparel of gorgeous dreams.
Day and night the doll as an angel is playing a fashion show
For us to enjoy.

日本料理店的海

我們三姊弟跳入海水裡
游泳唷！游泳
哈！哈！
我們抓了兩條魚
張大姐笑着說：誰抓我的腿啊！

誰．．最近我全家和張大哥及張小姐去吃飯，日本料理店的小房間裡之桌下，有一個和桌子同大的凹洞，那是給我們放腳用的，因為我國人不會像日本人一樣交足盤坐，坐在榻榻米上是無法吃飯的，因此，台灣的日本料理店的這種設計很理想。我看到這個有趣的洞，就說像跳入海中游泳一樣跳下去，在洞裡歡樂遊戲，並抓玩張小姐的腿，像抓了魚一樣，實在富於想像力，這首詩只是把我七歲的女兒當時講的極富詩意的話，寫下來而已。

142

At Sea at a Japanese Restaurant

We three sister and brothers jumped into the sea.
Swimming and swimming.
Ha, ha, ha.
We caught two fish.
Sister Zhang asked:
"Who caught my legs"

Note: One day, the Zhang family and my family visited a Japanese restaurant in Kaohsiung. We in Taiwan were not used to sitting on the tatami mat in a Japanese manner. To make us comfortable, they carved out the middle of tatami mat in the dining room in the shape of a circular hole for us to stretch our legs. The little children of our families imagined that the hole was like a sea. They began to play the game of catching fish. One of the children caught the legs of Miss Zhang. Out of the story, I wrote the poem for the children.

談兒童詩

(一)兒童詩的意義

有人概略地把「兒童詩」定義為「兒童寫的詩」和「給兒童讀的詩」及「適合兒童欣賞的詩」等，這是籠統而又正確的說法。

我想「兒童詩」也可以定義為「具有兒童靈魂及兒童意識的詩。也就是在感覺和知覺上，對事物及其意象，容易為兒童心靈感應的詩」，當然，這裡所說的事物，包括宇宙萬物的有形物及無形物，有形物如人、動物、花草、天空、太陽、星星等，無形物如時間、愛、恨、夢等，都包括在內；也包括萬物的存在和本質，如彩虹的麗色、美妙的鳥語、芬芳的花香和水蜜桃的甜味等。

簡單的「兒童詩」的定義，就像把「嬰兒奶粉」定義為「嬰兒吃的奶粉」一樣簡單明瞭，並沒有深入去探討為什麼嬰兒要吃嬰兒奶粉，其主要原因是沒有牙齒，所以沒有辦法像大人一樣吃飯和魚肉等，而嬰兒奶粉已經加入大部份嬰兒必需的蛋白質、脂肪、醣類、維他命和礦物質等，這些成份已經足夠維持嬰兒的營養，而不必去吃魚肉飯了。就像兒童只適合於讀兒童詩，不必去讀一般的古詩和現代詩（假如程度高，又有人指導的話，當然能夠讀這些詩是最好了），也不必研究保羅・梵樂希（Paul Valery）和T・S・艾略特（T・S・Eliot）等偉大詩人的詩和精闢入微的詩論一樣。

而成人也可以欣賞兒童詩，就像成人也可以吃嬰兒奶粉一樣。

也就是說,「兒童詩」是「兒童想出來的詩」。「成人替兒童創造出來的詩」也是「兒童詩」,因為成人也是由小孩長大而成的,當然,還保留著一些兒童的詩想,成人就是以他們仍保存著的兒童心靈創作兒童詩。

其有兒童心靈的成年詩人,因為具有成熟而豐富的學問、思想和經驗,因此,能夠寫出啟發兒童靈性和智慧的兒童詩,也能寫出感動兒童心靈和教育兒童思想及美德的兒童詩。

當然,兒童詩仍須具備一般詩的詩素,否則也不能成為兒童詩,它可以用平仄的古律詩體,也可以用自由的現代詩體,只是詩之內容和意象,要適合兒童的天性而已。

這好像玩具火車,小孩喜歡玩,成人也可以玩,它可以是小孩做出來的,也可以是大人做出來的,不管是誰做出來的,這個玩具火車的形象,必須具有真實的火車的一些外形,譬如,有火車的車頭、車廂和輪子等,就是構成一首詩的要素一樣,這些用鋼鐵或塑膠或木頭做成的玩具火車(好像兒童詩),必須做出像真實的火車頭、車廂和輪子的形象,小孩才會喜歡玩,就像具有詩素的兒童詩,被小孩喜歡讀、欣賞一樣。

成人可以去學開火車和玩玩具火車,就像小孩可以寫一般詩和兒童詩一樣,而小孩只能玩玩具火車,很難去學開火車,就像小孩只能寫兒童詩和欣賞兒童詩,很難寫出一般詩和欣賞一般詩一樣。因為一般詩的文字較艱難,用意深厚,思想既深又廣,創造的意象複雜龐大,意境巨大而遙遠,這是小孩感覺和思想不到的,就像很難讓小孩學開火車一樣,由於智力和體力之不足,要讓小孩正確駕駛不容易,速度很難控制,通行規則及

145

信號也難認清，對於緊急事故的應變能力不足，因此，只好去玩玩具火車了。

(二) 詩的意義

毛公的「詩大序」說：「詩有六義，一曰風、二曰賦、三曰比、四曰興、五曰雅、六曰頌。」周禮春官大師鄭注：「風，言賢聖治道之遺化；賦之言舖，直舖陳今之政教善惡；比，見今之失，不敢斥言，取比類以言之；興，見今之美，嫌於媚諛，取善事以喻勸之；雅，正也，言今之正者，以爲後世法；頌之言誦言，容也，誦今之德，廣以美之。」

這種詩的意義，頗符合社會教育的目的，也就是爲反映社會和表現社會而寫的「社會派的詩」，這種詩發揮了對社會的效用性，詩成爲社會教化的工具，使我們的社會成爲「溫柔敦厚」、具有「禮義廉恥」、「忠孝仁愛信義和平」的完善社會。

就詩的效用而言，詩是反映時代社會的文字音響，不但可以表達個人的心志，也可以反映一國的政治和風俗。譬如，由杜甫的春望：「國破山河在，城春草木深。感時花濺淚，恨別鳥驚心。烽火連三月，家書抵萬金。白頭搔更短，渾欲不勝簪。」可以感知當時戰亂之激烈，和通信之不易及內心之煩焦和痛苦。

由於兒童對國家的政風，沒有深入的瞭解和特殊的感觸，因此童詩裡面表現在這方面的很少。這也表示兒童雖然是國家未來的主人翁，但是，兒童的天真純潔的心靈還沒有被政治浸染，這是兒童心靈的可貴處，也是

146

童詩的一大特性。

但是，就詩的教育功能而言，成人應該多寫一些灌輸兒童正確的國家觀念和政治思想的詩來培養他們才好。

另外，就詩的本質和寫詩的靈感來源而言，是「詩言志」，也就是說，詩表現心裡的意識，以詩表達心裡所要講的一切東西。

事實上，不只是「詩」能夠「言志」，一般的說話，奉承或謾罵也是在「言志」，一切文學和藝術都能夠「言志」，散文可以直述言志；小說家可以透過自己製造出來的人物來表達自己的心意；畫家可以用色彩和線條，以視覺的語言，表現自己的思想；音樂家可以用五線譜、樂器和歌聲來表現自己的情意和思想；甚至，啞巴也可以用他的手勢來表達自己所要講的話，也就是「言志」。

因此，「言志」並非「詩」之獨有現象，只是「詩」「言志」之方法不同而已，而且，常常會有一首好詩之震撼力勝過一部小說或一場交響樂曲的現象。

詩的歌聲之亮麗僅次於音樂，詩的韻律和節奏，也僅次於音樂，而其美妙的幻想和敲擊心靈的響聲及深大高妙的意境和音樂相同，甚至有超越之處；而其構圖之明麗和意象之鮮活清新，也和繪畫一樣，甚至也有超越之處。還有，同一首樂曲，因演奏者不同，其表現的效果也不同，繪畫則更糟糕，其材料不管多麼優異，都會受自然風化的浸蝕剝離而變質脫落甚至腐壞，要永垂不朽是很難的，你看，歷史上的陽春白雪的古曲都沒有了，歷史上的許多古蹟古畫都消失了，而許多古文、古詩仍遺留到現在，現代的佳文和好詩也因為印在書上，就能夠保存得更久，一直留傳下去。

同樣是有價值的作品，文學就比音樂和繪畫更具有永久性。目前的兒童童詩之題材，大多是童心自然的流露，也就是「詩言志」，而且，小孩子寫的童詩之題材，大多是動物和較常看見的人物和東西，如蝴蝶、蜻蜓、孔雀、雞、鴨、長頸鹿、父母、老師、雨、雲、河、海、水、太陽、月亮、星星、汽球等。其寫法，大多以比喻性、趣味性、自我性和希望及夢想為主，他們寫了不少佳作，有些想像力極為豐富，令人稱奇，但是，思想上和技巧上，大多只變化了一層，很少有第二層或第三層甚至更多層的變化，有待更進一步努力。

保羅、梵樂希說：「詩是體驗的表現，詩人的目的，乃在與讀者作心靈的共鳴，和讀者共享神聖的一刻。」對小孩子而言，他們的生活體驗大多在「兒童樂園」、家庭、學校和同學之間，他們所要表現的，就是這個狹小的兒童範圍之內的感觸，他們能使讀者共鳴的東西，也大多侷限於此，只要詩寫得好，當然能夠和讀者共享神聖的一刻。而成人有過兒童時代的心靈和生活之體驗，也保留著一份孩童的赤子之心，當然，可以寫童詩給兒童和成人共鳴，且共享神聖的一刻。

(三) 兒童詩語言的問題

有人覺得寫兒童詩，要用很簡單的文字才好，因為兒童不懂得較專門性的和較深奧的語言和文字，我覺得並不儘然，因為任何學問都可以學習得來，學習多了，熟了，就變成小孩自己的知識和自己熟悉的語言，自然就會以這些專門名詞做為自己的語言來寫詩，而且，由於資訊的發達，自然

148

河

河流只有一條腸子

然科學及社會科學知識的普及，小孩學習能力的提高，對於新鮮的名詞和字眼，只要多解說幾次，多背幾次，就能夠明瞭熟悉。

譬如，一年級的小學生，在幼稚園時，一個中文字都沒有學過，到了讀一年級時，只讀了幾個月，就懂得而且會寫不少的中文字，甚至很難寫的字，例如，「還」、「聽」等。而且，小學課程的自然科學裡，也有一些現在的高中和大學生不懂的內容，但是，年紀小小的小學生被老師一教就會了。

因此，所謂簡單或困難，只是有沒有去教，有沒有去學習而已，教得好，學習得熟悉就變成簡單了，反之，若不教又不學，就很困難了。

當然，困難度也是有一個層次的，譬如，教一個普通的小學生學習微積分是不可能的（當然也有一些天才兒童可以），這是因為微積分比起一般數學的層次高得很多，很難被兒童理解。

而成人寫的童詩，對兒童的心靈和詩想之啟發很重要，許多小孩寫的詩，在題材和用語上，都多多少少受過大人寫的童詩和童話的影響，好像大人牽手帶小孩走過獨木橋一樣，第二次小孩就會自己走了。當然，也有小孩自己跟朋友玩一玩，就會走獨木橋的。

為了進一步說明兒童詩語言的問題，我列舉我在台灣時報發表的童詩「河」，來析釋一下：

婉婉蠕動著
她吃得不多
永遠是苗條細長的

很多人喜歡這首詩，但是，最近有位師專剛畢業的老師認為「蠕動」不是小孩子用的語言，因為小孩子懂得的和想得出的語言很簡單。我覺得他只說對了一半，因為小孩用的語言雖然很簡單，但是經過教導和學習，就能夠進入更深層的語言世界，熟悉了這個較深層的語言世界之後，就能夠操作這些語言了。

譬如，「聽」是用耳朵聽聲音，「跳」是用腳跳起來，這是一般兒童都知道的用語。

而「蠕動」是「昆蟲行動的樣子」，這個語言可能比較難，但是，如果讓兒童看一下蚯蚓和蠶行動的樣子，並教導他們說，這就叫做「蠕動」這個語言的形象，再告訴他們身體裡面腸子運動的情形，就建立了「蠕動」這個語言流比喻為腸子的語言，就可以感覺出蠕動的意味了。到這時候，經成為兒童的語言，當他看見昆蟲的蠕動，而將河因為腸子在身體裡面看不見，但是，經過這樣教導之後，他們也能夠想像得出腸子的蠕動樣子，或者藉塑膠製的腸子活動模型也可以瞭解，當然最好是用醫學的映片放映出來看看，就最清楚了。經過這樣的教育之後作文或寫詩時，「蠕動」這個語言用上去，以後在語文的訓練上，碰到恰當的情況，他就會把「蠕動」這個語言永久留在兒童的記憶之中，以後作文或寫詩時，就上升了一層，在「詩語」和「詩想」上，也提昇了更高的層次。

150

目前兒童詩大多內涵不夠深厚廣大的最大原因，就是兒童在文字的認識上訓練不夠，因此，「詩語」的來源不足，不易開拓深厚廣大的「詩想」意境。

因此，要開拓和發展更高層次的童詩，最主要的是「詩語」（詩的語言）之教導和訓練及運用，以開拓和啟發「詩想」的流動，展向深厚廣大的境界裡去。

而詩是淨化過的語言，不管怎樣簡單的語言，也要淨化為詩語之後，才能成為詩，不管兒童詩、少年詩或一般的成人詩，都是如此。

至於，較少用的或較艱深的文字和語言，只要適合他表現的思想和形象，經過淨化之後，也能夠成為兒童詩語。

假如，把我這首童詩「河」，列入二、三年級的國語課本中，只要老師一教，學生馬上就會懂，而且，很快能夠記憶起來。這首詩不但可以啟發兒童的詩之想像力，而且，富有詩之趣味性和哲理性。

當然，童詩「詩語」之芳香、味道、音感、色感、形象和意念，必須適合兒童才恰當，像養樂多為兒童喜歡一樣，養樂多就成為兒童的飲料和「詩語」，而威士忌和高梁酒，只適於成人飲用，而不能成為兒童的飲料，雖然，也有大人喜歡喝養樂多的，就像有些大人仍喜歡欣賞兒童詩一樣，這是正常的現象，因為在生理上和心理上，大人是由兒童演變過來的，還遺留著兒童的雛型。

(四) 舉例

由於我國教育的發達，印刷出版業的驚人發展、公私機關團體的獎勵及社會各界人士對兒童文學的關心，使我國在兒童文學方面有很大的進展，雖然，距離理想仍很遠，但是，我深信前途很樂觀。

很多小孩都有極天真可愛的詩想和驚人的詩語出現，很可惜很少人把它們記載下來，兒童自己不去記載，父母親也懶得去記載，結果，像一陣風一吹就走了，無影無蹤地飄逝了，我勸做父母的及兄姊和老師們，一有機會應該把小孩說出的詩語和詩想記載下來。而認得字的小朋友們則應該努力把它們記載下來。

最近，小孩子寫的詩很多，發表在報紙和雜誌上的也不少，有些寫得相當好。

現在，我舉一些例子來說明：

鐘

　　　　　　台中縣僑仁國小
　　　　　　六年級　林純如

小小的房間裏
住著高矮不齊的房客
每天不停地工作
難道它們不會累嗎

我覺得這首詩寫得很好，在短短的四行裡，表現了詩之知性、感性、趣味性和天真的同情心。

——原載74年10月20日中華兒童

他以天真可愛的詩心，認識了鐘的實體，透視了它的存在和活動的本質與其真諦。

林同學把「鐘」比喻為「小小的房間」，這是很好的比喻，裏面「住著高矮不齊的房客」，即鐘內有秒針、分針和時針，他將這三種長短不同的針擬人化，而成為「高矮不齊的房客」，他不再用「長短」，而用「高矮」是很上乘的。他又把針的轉動，活化為「每天不停地工作」，實在太妙了。

小 河

北市蓬萊國小　六之三　鄭振牟

小河是位長舌婦，
他有說不完的話題，
從上游說到海洋，
從上古說到現代，
日復一日，年復一年，
永遠的說下去……。

——原載74年10月14日中央日報兒童週刊

這首詩極富創意，小河婉蜒不停的流動，產生潺潺不息的流聲，像「長舌婦」說話不停，比喻甚佳，是極鮮活的意象，有透視過的親切實感。又把從上游流到海，說成「從上游說到海洋」，也比喻得很好，很有連貫

153

性。而且，鄭同學也知道小河的生命很古老，自從上古就已經形成，到現在還流著，天天流著；像「永遠的說下去⋯⋯」一樣，像尼羅河或黃河或恆河一樣，在他小小的心靈裡，也有永恆不息的時間觀念，爲極佳的想像。

可惜用錯了一個字，就是第二行要用「她」而不該用「他」，因爲長舌婦是女人。

時　間

屏縣光華國小
五年甲班　莊永慶

時間是個無情漢，
一但過去了，
怎樣呼喚，
也不回頭看一看。

——原載笠67期

這首詩比喻得很好，意象鮮活，也用了一些韻，是好詩。可惜，第二行的「一但」，應改爲「一旦」才對。

這首詩有成人的想法存在，却出自五年級的小學生的腦裡，可見其思想較一般學童成熟得多。

154

孔雀

屏縣光華國小 四年級 徐久仁

孔雀一定很怕熱
不然怎麼會
在屁股上裝上一枝大扇子呢？

——原載笠62期

這首詩的想法極為天真可愛，他很可能在天氣炎熱時，到屏東公園看了孔雀開屏後發想出來的妙詩。

一般孩子喜歡看孔雀，是因為孔雀漂亮，開屏的動作很有趣，開屏後更漂亮；而徐同學卻想到孔雀的尾巴羽毛像大扇子，以便自我搖扇，解除暑熱，是很好的想法。

我想第三行「裝上」的「上」可以不要，以免與「屁股上」的「上」重複，又可以更簡練些。

小丑

宜蘭二城國小 五年級 尤惠君

小丑，小丑
紅紅的鼻子
亮亮的眼睛

他逗我們笑 誰來逗他笑

──原載風箏第二期

小丑是逗人笑的戲子，大多小丑身世可憐，生活貧困。他却隱藏着滿腹的辛酸，做出各式各樣的語態，來觀眾歡笑，却無人來逗他笑，只有五年級的尤同學已經知道小丑的可憐，在觀戲之餘，還萌出「誰來逗他笑」的憐憫之心，實在可貴。

尺

尺是忠厚的小孩，
總是走直路，
不走歪路。

苗栗海寶國小 六年級 陳 錦

──原載布穀鳥第一期

這是一首極富教育性的童詩，成人如果寫得出這首詩就不錯了，何況是小學生寫的，實在難能可貴。陳同學能夠把枯燥的計算數理的尺，比喻為忠厚的小孩，在意象上、哲理上，趣味上和教育上，都是第一流的詩法。它「總是走直路，不走歪路」，實在講得太好了。

156

另外，再舉一首外國兒童寫的詩：

星

日本東京都
小島小學六年　武井美智子

在黑暗的太空有兩顆閃亮的光
那是星星
在那小星中好像鑲有一玻璃珠
星星在放射通信網
好像又有一個世界

——原載「小學生詩の本」

這首詩之可貴處，在於創造了科幻的詩之世界。「星星在放射通信網，好像又有一個世界。」這是以具有科學知識的詩語，創造出來的科幻詩之世界。

現代詩裡用了許多科技用語，是很多人都知道的。但是，小學生能夠這樣用得恰到好處，實在不簡單。這是我國兒童值得學習的地方。

(5) 結　語

由此可知，基本上，兒童詩的創作方法和詩素，跟一般詩差不多，只是其語言和意象較富童性之意趣而已。

75年8月　心臟詩刊

Children's Poetry:

1. The Meaning of Children's Poetry

Children's poetry can be defined as follows: Poetry written by children, poetry written for children and poetry fit for children. The definition seems to be imprecise yet correct.

However, I would like to define it: Poetry that takes children's soul and that which appeals to children as its content in being able to touch children emotionally and intellectually through concrete images and cognition of the things around them. Here, the things around them should be taken to indicate those that are visible and invisible in the cosmos. The visible are: humans, animals, the sky, the sun, the stars, etc. The invisible are: time, love, hate, dreams, etc. The above includes being and essence of all: the color of the rainbow, the melody of chirping birds, the fragrance of blooming flowers and the sweetness of peaches.

If we simply define children's poetry as we might define babies' milk as milk for babies, we cannot fully understand why the milk is fit for babies to drink. If we look more carefully into why the milk is called babies' milk, we would find the fact that they drink the milk because they are toothless and they cannot take in rice, fish, meat, etc. as adults do. Furthermore, in the milk, nutrients such as proteins, fats, carbohydrates, vitamins, minerals, etc. are added to sustain the life and growth of the babies. With them, they don't have to eat rice, etc. as adults do. Generally speaking, children read children's poetry, not the poetry by such poets as Paul Valery or T. S. Eliot. They are not well prepared for the difficult poetry like world classics or modern poetry. Of course, there are a select few who can read it at an early age, but this is rare.

On the other hand, the adults can read children's poetry. In the same manner, they can also drink babies' milk.

The ideas in children's poetry are conceived out of the children's mind. In writing children's poetry, an adult author harbors children's mind. William Wordsworth (1770-1850) says, "The child is father of the man" in his "My Heart Leaps up":

My heart leaps up when I behold
A rainbow in the sky:
So was it when my life began;
So it is now I am a man;
So be it when I shall grow old,
Or let me die!
The child is father of the man;
And I could wish my days to be
Bound each to each by natural piety

Truly, adults used to be children. They still keep some memories of things past in their childhood. The memories help them in their writing of children's poetry. In other words, children's poetry is conceived and written by children and / or adults who have grown out of children.

In addition to having children's mind, the adults write their poetry out of their ideas, experiences and knowledge of life. They are able to write children's poetry to enlighten children's mind and wisdom in order that they might move children and educate them.

To write children's poetry, some ingredients are supposed to be used in it. Some poetic forms and contents suitable for children should be used. Let us take toy trains for example in writing children's poetry. Toy trains can be made by adults or children. In any event, they should be like real trains: the locomotive, the cars, the wheels, etc. These give images of a real train, and they are the ingredients that constitute a train. The matter that is used in the toy trains can be steel, wood, or plastic; yet, the form is there. The form of the toy trains invites children to play with them. In the same manner, children's poetry should be written with ingredients of poetry so much so that it may invite children's to read it.

Adults can devise and make toy trains; they can also drive real trains. Adults can write children's poetry and poetry for the general reading public. On the other hand, children can only play toy trains and they are not supposed to drive real trains. Of course, they read children's poetry and they may themselves write children's poetry. They are not supposed to write poetry for the general reading public as T. S. Eliot or Paul Valery did in their poetry. Poems written by them contain complexity in forms, ideas, contents, images and language. As mentioned above, children are not supposed to operate a real train because they are not physically and intellectually fit for the job. They are not ready to deal with complicated mechanism of train piloting and regulations governing train traffic and accidents on the rails.

2. the Meaning of Poetry

In a Preface to the Book of Odes, Maestro Mao says: "Poetry has six functions, Feng (風), Fu (賦), Bi (比), Xing (興), Ya (雅) and Song (頌)."According to the Spring Minister of the Zhou Dynasty, "Feng means a narration of the governance of the sages. Fu means a deliberation of the good and evil of contemporary politics. Bi means comparison, a comparison and criticism of the recent politics with the previous one without directly attacking the weaknesses committed by the present dministration. There is just comparison calling for the ministers' attention to the weaknesses of their administration. Xing means pointing out the good the ministers have done to the people without flattery and advising them to continually do the same. Ya means uprightness, urging the ministers to set good examples for the posterity. Song means recitation of the present good governance calling the ministers to set good examples for the later generations."

The main thesis of poetry at this early age, the Shang and the Zhou Dynasties, in Chinese history is one about politics, education and society. Poetry is functional in that the people should be educated to behave and the ministers should be urged to govern well. That kind of society is full of gentleness, and honesty, and courtesy, justice, cleanness and a sense of shame. In short, the community should be one of loyalty between the governor and the governed, filial piety paid by children to their parents, faith in the ministers shown by the people, justice in human relations and benevolence and love shown among neighbors. Thus, society would a peaceful one. In conclusion, poetry should play the role of bringing an ideal world for the people to live in. This concept in Chinese political culture is Shijie Datong (世界大同).

Poetry can be an echo of the times' resounding voices. In it, one's will and feeling about the politics and customs of a society can be the content of a poem. Let's take Du Fu's (杜甫; 712–770) "The Spring View"(春望) for example:

Though a country be sundered, hills and rivers endure;
And spring comes green again to trees and grasses
Where petals have been shed like tears
And lonely birds have sung their grief.
After the war-fires of three months,
One message from home is worth a ton of gold.
I stroke my white hair. It has grown too thin
To hold the hairpins any more.

> —Translated by Harold Witter Bynner, also known by the nom de plume Emanuel Morgan, (August 10, 1881–June 1, 1968), an American poet and translator.

In the above-mentioned poem, we see the speaker of the poem's pains and worries about his war-torn country where communication with others is difficult.

It is difficult to see the same thing in children's poetry today. It seems that the poetry does not take as content matters concerning politics and government. Children, the future masters of the country, do not generally show interest in them. It seems that children are not yet contaminated by them. That is one of the main features of children's poetry. Yet, the adults who are citizens of a country should imbue children with some proper ideas of the society and country they live in.

As far as the nature and the inspiration of poetry-writing are concerned, one's will / intention can be the primary force behind poetry-writing. The poetic discourse is the instrument the poet uses to voice his will / intention vis-a-vis the world out there. In fact, other discourses such as daily conversation in the forms of swearing and flattery also express one's will / intention. Prose and novels may function in the same way. Painters use lines and shades of colors and composers, musical notes to do the same. Even the mute can use their gestures and facial / bodily expressions to speak out their emotions, etc.

In expressing the will, poetry is not the only way, but it is a different way. Sometimes, poetry can speak better than other forms. That is why a poem may speak louder than a novel or a symphony. The melody and rhythm of poetry stand next to those of music. The fantasy, the sounds touching the mind and the fresh images of poetry can be similar to those of music. Sometimes, poetry can do better than music. The composition of bright and fresh images in poetry can be the same as in painting. Sometimes, poetry can do better than paintings. On the other hand, a player or a director may interpret differently a piece of music. Great paintings would not endure the corrosion of time. It is unlikely for them to remain fresh through time.

Many of musical compositions have been forgotten, and historic spots and art pieces have been destroyed by time. It seems that only literary works endure. Poetic works endure better than either music or paintings.

Recent children's poetry is one about children's overflow of their spontaneous emotions. Children's poetry is about children's will and feeling of things around them: butterflies, dragonflies, phoenixes, chickens, ducks, giraffes, parents, teachers, rain, clouds, rivers, the sea, water, the sun, the moon, stars, balloons, etc. Children write about them mostly in funny comparisons about how they think of them in their hopes and probably in dreams. In the poetry, we find there is strong imagination; yet, their thinking and skill of wielding language remain on the rudimental stage, rarely reaching something far beyond that. It seems that they should be trained to write something more profound.

Paul Valery says, "Poetry is a performance of experience. The aim of poetry is to communicate with its readers and share a holy moment with them." Children's life is limited in the playground, the home and family, the school and their relationships with their friends. What they feel about is limited. Their poetry is about their limited experiences here. Still, they can write about them in their poetry. They can share their holy moment with their readers. Adults used to be children. They can go back to some of their experiences they have had as children. I believe that they can write poetry for children out of children's mind they still keep. The poetry they write may be read by children and adults as well.

3. The Problem Concerning Language in Children's Poetry

It is said that children's poetry should be written in simple language because children are not prepared to read complex and difficult language. I cast doubt on this point. Children can be trained to read it and take it as their own. If they are used to it through reading and training, they can use it in their own poetry writing.

Ours is an information society; children are exposed to all kinds of data in natural and social sciences. New ideas and language are there; children can take them as their own. There, they can learn and be trained to learn. A first-year student at a primary school, not having learned many Chinese words in kindergarten, learns some from the media. Children are taught to learn not some words but also some knowledge of natural and social sciences. Teaching them to learn to know some language and facts about the world would solve the problem of simplicity and complexity of language. In short, if we teach children to learn, they would be able to use words and knowledge to read and write their own poetry.

Indeed, it is difficult to teach average primary-school students to learn calculus. Of course, there are some exceptionally gifted ones who can be taught and learn this advanced discipline in mathematics. Much of it is incomprehensible to them. Children should be taught step by step. Learning is a key to solve the problem of simplicity and complexity of language and knowledge.

The first job for an adult poet to write poetry for children is to enlighten their mind to ideas of poetry. Children who write poetry may have been influenced by poetry written by the adults. It is like grown-ups leading the little ones to walk on a narrow wooden bridge. Having walked on it the first time, they will do the same on themselves the second time. Of course, a group of children playing together would also learn to cross the river on the wooden bridge.

To illustrate how to solve the problem of the language in children's poetry, I shall give a poem by myself as an example published in the Taiwan Times below:

The River
The river is like an intestine,
Winding and squirming (蠕動).
She does not eat much.
She is always slim and long.

Many like the little poem. A teacher fresh from a teachers' college said that winding and squirming (蠕動) are difficult for children to comprehend and are seldom used by them. For him, children's language should be simple and easy. It seems to me that it is true that children's language should be simple and easy. Through teaching and learning, however, children should be able to know some advanced words. Having learnt them, children should be able to use them in their own poetry.

Words like hearing and jumping are familiar to children. Winding and squirming which describe the manner of the motion of worms are quite foreign to children. If they are invited to observe some earthworms and silkworms, they would be able to see what the expression would mean and they would visualize the motion of the intestines in our body. The teaching can be done through pictures, charts, models and / or short films. Then, they would be able to compare the motion of the river to that of an intestine. Winding and squirming would be part of the corpus of their language. In their reading and writing, the expression would be familiar to them. In such a way, their learning would arrive at a higher stage.

It seems to me that there is a problem in children's poetry today. The width and profundity of it remain to be improved. The problem lies in the inadequacy of training of children's recognition of vocabulary. As a result, their knowledge of poetic language is not enough to express their will and intention in their poetry in a wide and profound manner.

The problem of writing children's poetry of a higher quality lies in that of the poetic language used in it. Children can be educated in its recognition and its employment. Then, children's poetic ideas would be explored, and they would fluently find their way in the writing and reading of poetry. Furthermore, poetic language is a purified form of it. Language, however simple, should be purified to find its way in poetry, children's poetry or poetry for the general reader. Difficult or rarely used words, after having been purified, can also be used in children's poetry. If we put "The River" as a reading in the curriculum in the second or the third year of primary school and if the teacher acquaints the students with the difficult language and ideas, then the poem would help the students know the vocabulary and the images in it. The poem would be full of interest and philosophical ideas for the students.

The fragrance, taste, sound, sense of colors, images and intention of a poem should suit children. Yakuludo, a drink, is welcome to children; it is their drink like children's poetry. Whisky and gaoliang (a Chinese strong liquor) are not children's drink; they are the adults'. The adults drink not only whisky and gaoliang but also yakuludo. Similarly, they read poetry for the general public and children's poetry. The adults read children's poetry because psychological and physiologically, sympathetically and empathetically, they can comprehend the language and the images in it. The adults have grown out of children. They still keep children's mind.

4. More Examples

Under the present situation of the fast development of our education and our printing industry and great encouragement from the government and the private sectors, children's literature has made great progress.

I believe that there is still room for more progress.

Many children have their lovable and innocent ideas for poetry which can be fit for poetic language, but very few people would record them. If the children do not track them down and their parents would not do the same, the above would disappear like a gust of wind. I would like to suggest that adults, parents or teachers, take down the children's works and that the children themselves do the same.

Now, let me take the chance to examine some examples:

The Clock
In a little room,
There live tenants of different heights.
They work endlessly every day.
Don't they get tired?
— Lin Chunru, a sixth-year student, Qiaoren Primary School, Taichong. Zhonghua Children's Magazine, October 20, 1985.

It seems to me it is a well-written poem. We find children's sense and sensibility, interest and innocent compassion in it. She observes the object of the clock from her innocent mind. She examines the value of its existence and its function. Her comparison of the clock to a little room is appropriate. She also compares the three hands, those of hour, minute and second, to tenants of different heights / lengths. She uses heights instead of lengths, which is very good to me. She personifies the clock, and its moving to working endlessly every day. In the poem, rhetoric techniques such as denotation, connotation, metaphor, simile and personification can be found.

The Little River
The little river is
Like a gossiping woman.
She has a lot of topics to talk about
All the way from upstreams down to the sea,
From time immemorial down to the present.
Day and night, year after year,
She talks on and on.
—Zheng Zhenmou, a sixth-year student, Fenglai Primary School, Taipei.
—Children's Weekly, the Zhongyang Newspaper, October 14, 1985.

The poem is full of creative thinking. The winding river flows endlessly producing endless sounds like a gossiping woman talking all the time. The images are fresh. The simile is to the point where the river is compared to a gossiping woman. In considering the image, Zheng deliberates the problems of space and time. The motif of never ending is there in the poem, calling our attention to bigger rivers such as the Nile River in Egypt and the Yellow River in China, both the birthplaces of ancient civilizations. Indeed, the idea of time's endlessness is connected to that of the river flowing is one of good imagination.

There is a weakness in the Chinese version of the poem. In referring to the river as a gossiping woman, Zheng used he instead of she. The antecedent in the text is feminine; its pronoun should rhetorically be feminine.

Time
Time is a ruthless man.
Having once disappeared,
However hard you try to call him
He would not turn back.
　— Zhuang Yongqing, a fifth-year student, Guanghua Primary School,
　　Pingdong. The Li Journal for Poetry, #67.

Here, we find a good metaphor. The comparison is fresh and vivid. The child's imagination is as mature as that of an adult. Don't say children do not have any power of imagination.

The Phoenix
The phoenix should be afraid of heat;
Otherwise, why is there a big fan
Equipped on its buttocks?
　— Xu Jiuren, a fourth-year student, Guanghua Primary School, Pingdong.

The Li Journal for Poetry, #62.

In the poem, we find the child's imagination is fun and interesting. He could have visited Pingdong Park in summer. He projected his feeling of sultriness of summer on to the phoenix. Children like to watch a phoenix open its tail which is like a big fan. In the hot season of summer, the child associate the open tail to a big fan to cool itself. The comparison is apt for me.

The Clown
Oh, clown, oh clown,
You have a red nose and
Twinkling eyes.
You try to make us laugh.
Who would make you laugh?
—You Huijun, a fifth-year student, Ercheng Primary School, Ilan. Fengzheng, #2.

Clowns' job is to make the audience laugh in a circus. Many of them come from humble families. They have undergone all kinds of difficulties; yet, they hide them, but they try to please the audience with their speech and body language. Who can please them? Student You finds out their problem—their pitiable situation. Off the stage, the child asks, "Who would make you laugh?"

The Ruler
The ruler is a silly and honest child.
He always walks on a straight road,
Not on a crooked one.
   — Chen Jin, a sixth-year student, Haibao Primary School, Miaoli.
   — The Cuckoo Bird, #1.

This is an educative poem. It is rare for a primary-school student to use such a personification. The personification is excellent for the child poet. An adult would not think of it in his writing. It is interesting for Student Chen to compare the ruler to a silly and honest child. The method, personification, is philosophically and educationally appropriate. The lines, "He always walks on a straight road, / Not on a crooked one" are well written.

Let us examine a poem by a Japanese student.

The Stars
In the dark sky, there are two shining balls.
They are stars.
They look like being studded with glass beads.
They seem to be radiating a communication network.
It suggests that there could be another world out there.
—Tageiyi Mijiko, a sixth-year student, Kojima Primary School, Tokyo, Japan.

The child uses the idea of science fiction in her poetic imagination. The lines, "They seem to be radiating a communication network. / It suggests that there could be another world out there." In her imagination, she has created a world of science fiction.

It is well known that in modern poetry, vocabulary of science and technology is widely used, but it is rare for a child poet to use it. We here in Taiwan have a lot to learn from her.

5. Conclusion

From the above, it is clear that children's poetry is no different from other poetry as far as its creation and poetic elements are concerned. The only difference is that language and images in children's poetry should suit the need of children.
—The Heart Journal for Poetry, August 1986.

父母捕捉兒童詩語

兒童的心靈是純潔的,兒童的語言是天真的。

我想許多父母親,都曾經聽過自己的小孩,說出像詩、像寓言、像童話或像圖畫般美妙的語句,令大人們驚訝讚絕不已,但是,很少父母親會把自己小孩的如此美妙的詩句記載下來,然而,這些妙語,就像忽然出現的絕妙靈感一樣,你如果不把這個靈感馬上寫出來,它會像一陣煙一樣,立即飛逝,實在可惜。

我自己雖然寫詩,但是,我的小孩偶然講出的「詩語」,比我寫的詩還好,所以我記載了起來。

以下是她的「詩語」:

我的女孩玉佩,民國67年7月出生,現就讀七賢國小幼稚園。

(1)民國71年中秋節晚上,美麗的月亮,高掛在高雄的天空上,玉佩看了圓圓的月亮好高興,她說:「月亮像一個大球,高飛在天空上。」當天晚上,在高雄遊玩後,我開車載妻和她回屏東鄉下,到了故鄉,玉佩抬頭一望,看到月亮,很高興地說:「月亮跟我們回到故鄉了。」

(2)民國72年3月,南台灣的春色迷人,綠意盎然,我載妻子、小男孩榮廷和玉佩到屏東縣歷史最悠久的萬金莊天主堂去玩,因車行近山,沿途所見,盡是綠色山脈。

玉佩問:「爸爸,車子能不能夠開過山的那邊去?」

我答:「山很高,開不過去。」

玉佩很機智地說:「把山用刀子剖開來,像剖西瓜一樣,車子就可以開過去了。」真是比愚公移山的故事還富詩意。

171

(3)民國73年2月,玉佩看了彎彎的月亮,說:「月亮像指甲。」

(4)民國73年3月,玉佩指著自己家門前的汽車說:「爸爸的車子又醒了,現在載我們出去玩。」她把無生命的汽車,擬化為牛馬之類的動物來載人,實在有趣。

其次,我覺得人與人之間的感情,本來是很真摯的,這可由玉佩(二歲半)和弟弟(一歲)在一起時,流露出的天真感情表現出來,茲舉三個例子來看看:

① 玉佩搖弟弟睡覺

玉佩的手搖著搖籃說:
「弟弟,我的搖籃給你睡,
弟弟,姊姊給你搖搖籃,
弟弟,姊姊給你搖搖籃,
弟弟,乖乖,姊姊給你搖搖籃,
弟弟,睡睡,
弟弟,睡睡……」
弟弟就閉眼睡了。

② 給銅板

玉佩說:「.爸爸,把銅板給我。」
我給了她兩個銅板。
玉佩說:「一個給弟弟好嗎?」

172

我說：「好！妳很疼愛妳的弟弟，妳很乖！」

玉佩就給了一個小銅板給小弟弟。

③ 有魔鬼

玉佩問：「爸爸，外面很黑暗，會有挖人心肝的魔鬼，是嗎？」

我說：「是的。」

小弟弟不懂事，打開門就出去了。

玉佩忙抓小弟弟，抓不住，哭了。

她哭着說：「弟弟會被魔鬼帶走的。」

另外，我再寫兩首詩，以表達我對女兒玉佩（兩歲半）和兒子榮廷（一歲多）之親情。（當時為70年春天）

(一) 給吾女玉佩

佩佩看星星
星星亮晶晶
佩佩看蝴蝶
蝴蝶吻花飛
佩佩看小鳥

小鳥吱吱叫
佩佩盪鞦韆
鞦韆像搖籃
佩佩喲！佩佩
人生只開一次花蕊

(二) 給吾兒榮廷

只識多多
只知喝奶
不識風吹雨落
不知天高地厚
願你是一條昇龍
飛向太陽
燃燒你自己照
照亮環宇
廿一世紀屬於你
願你高舉勝利旗幟

註：多多即養樂多

74年4月14日　台灣時報

Some Children's Poetic Language a Father Has Captured

The mind of children is pure, and their language is innocent.

As parents, we may have heard our children speak amazing remarks like those found in poetry, fables, fairy tales or pictures. We may be surprised, but very few parents would track them down in their notebooks. If we do not write them down, they would disappear like a gust of wind.

I write poetry. My three children occasionally speak out some poetic sentences. I keep them down because, it seems to me, they are better than mine.

My daughter, Yupei, born in July 1978, is studying at the Kindergarten, Qixian Primary School. Her poetic discourses are as follows:

At the mid-Autumn Festival in 1982, a gorgeous moon is hung on the sky in Kaohsiung. she was happy at seeing the moon there. She remarked, "The moon is like a big balloon flying high in the sky." On the same night, after we had had fun in Kaohsiung, I drove the whole family back to Pingdong. After stepping out of the car and looking up at the moon, she once again said, "The moon has followed us back to our homeland."

In March 1983, spring in southern Taiwan was fascinating. I took my wife, my son Rongting and Yupei to visit the historic Wanjinzhuang Cathedral in Pingdong County. We were approaching the Cathedral amidst green mountains.

Yupei asked "Can we drive our car over the mountains to the other side?"
I answered, "The mountains are too high to cross them."
She wittily commented, "We may cut them down with a knife like a watermelon. Then the car would cross them."

The remark is as powerful and poetic as the fable of Yugong Yishan (A foolish father trying to move the mountain in a Chinese fable).

In February 1984, seeing a crescent in the sky, she commented, "The moon is like the white of a fingernail."

In March 1984, pointing at the car near the front door, Yupei said, "Father's car has come back to life and is going to take us for an outing." It is interesting for her to compare a lifeless machine to an ox or a horse. She was personifying the car to an animal. The device of personification is a technique in poetry-writing.

Through the interaction between sister (Yupei) aged two and a half and brother(Rongting) aged one, I see true passion there. There are three examples:

Yupei Is Rocking the Cradle with Her Brother in it to Sleep

Yupei was rocking the cradle and said,
"Little brother, I am rocking the cradle for you to go to sleep;
Little brother, your big sister is rocking the cradle;
Little brother, be obedient, your big sister is rocking the cradle;
Little brother, sleep, little brother, sleep...."
And the little brother slept.

Giving Coins

Yupei asked, "Give me some coins."
I gave her two.
She asked, "May I give one to my little brother?"
I answered, "OK, you are good and you love your little brother."
Yupei gave one to her little brother.

There is a Devil

Yupei said,
    "It is dark outside. Is there a devil who might dig out one's heart and liver?"
I answered, "Yes."

Her little brother, knowing nothing about the world, opened the door and
    rushed out.
She failed to catch her little brother and cried.
She said, "He would be taken away by the devil."

Two more poems there are about the passion between Yupei and her little brother Rongting in the spring of 1981 as follows.

For My Daughter Yupei

Yupei is looking at the stars;
The stars are blinkering.
Yupei is looking at the butterflies;
They dance and kiss the flowers.
Yupei is looking at the little birds and
They are chirping.
Yupei is playing the swing
Like shaking in a cradle.
Oh, Yupei, Oh, Yupei,
Life is like a flower which blooms only once.

For My Son Rongting

You know nothing about the world,
Nor do you know the wind and the rain.
What you do know is drinking milk
And yakuluto.

I wish you to be like a dragon
Flying high to the sun and
To burn yourself to brighten the universe.

The twenty-first century would belong to you and
You would raise a banner signifying your victory.

   —Taiwan Times, April 14, 1985.

〈兒童文學家傳記〉

格林兄弟 二人合一

一、生於戰爭之中

以格林童話揚名於世的格林兄弟，兄叫雅哥夫·格林（Jacob Grimm，1785－1863），弟叫維爾漢·格林（Wilhelm Grimm，1786－1859）。他們生於德國中部黑森省的哈淄市，他們的父親是律師。哥哥十一歲的時候，父親就因為肺炎死了。而後，母親艱苦地養育了六個孩子，經過了法國革命和同盟戰爭等戰亂時期。很幸運地，這時獲得母親的姊姊之援助，格林兄弟始得進入卡斯爾古典高級中學，去讀法律系，但是，經由恩師沙維尼（F. C. V. Savigny, 1779 — 1861）的介紹，認識了同時代的作家布仁坦諾（C. Brentano，1778－1842）和阿爾寧（A. V. Arnim），而改變了他們以後一生的生活。

二、著書不凡

一八一一年，兄雅哥夫·格林出版了處女作「古代德國的師傅之歌」（Über den altdentschen Meistergesang），弟弟維爾漢也翻譯出版了「古代丹麥的英雄歌、民謠和故事」。他們兩兄弟之所以會開始研究德國和日耳曼的古代文學，是因為得到阿爾寧的啟示和身受拿破

178

崙軍隊佔領首都的感觸而引起的,並想由此研求過去的基層文化的精神根基。次年,一八一二年十二月他們出版了第一部「兒童和家庭的童話」(Kinder- und Hausmarchen 或譯為「格林童話集」),這時候,他們兄弟都還很年輕,兄廿七歲,弟廿六歲,這是由世界的故事研究為出發點,而寫出的歷史性的偉大作品。

兄雅哥夫為了維護病弱的弟弟維爾漢和其他弟妹的生活,他做了很多不稱心的工作,一八一三年,他當過外交官,次年,弟維爾漢也當了黑森省的選帝侯圖書館的書記(選帝侯是在中世紀德意志帝國有資格選舉皇帝的七個諸侯)。兩年後,兄雅哥夫和一起來這圖書館任職,在這裡,他們就能夠共同專心研究文學了。這時,他們出版了「德國傳說集」(Deutsche Sagen, 1816—1818)。次年,一八一九年雅哥夫出版了劃時代的第一部「德文文法」(Deutsche Grammatik),對日耳曼語的子音推移,也就是格林法則的說明和對語言學的研究有很大的貢獻。雅哥夫研究很勤,他終生收集徹底而完全的資料來寫作,並出版了「德國法律古事誌」(Deutsche Rechtsaltertumer, 1828)和「德國神話學」(Deutsche Mythologie, 1835)。

一八二九年,維爾漢發表了「德國英雄傳說」(Deutsche Helden-sage)之後,兄弟兩人被隣近的哈諾華省的哥登根大學聘請去當教授,也就是格林法則的說明和對語言學的研究有很大的貢獻。兩人居住在卡斯爾的弟弟路德比夫的家。為了打破經濟上的困境,他們兄弟兩人打算編集「德文辭典」(Deutsches Worterbuch),但是,這部辭典必需化費一百年以上的時間才寫得完,也就是說要到一九六一年,才能完成。一八四〇年,兄弟兩人被柏

校大學聘請去任教，因此，他到了五十幾歲，才開始著手編輯這部辭典，終於在一八五四年，出版了第一冊。

三、兄弟情深和睦

格林兄弟兩人的性格是不同的，兄獨身，終生不婚，弟有結婚。兄的性格是理知性的，而弟是文學性的，因此，成了奇妙的對比，然而，兄弟極為和睦，幾乎一輩子都在同一家庭生活着。他們寫的「兒童和家庭的童話」及「德國傳說集」等初期的六種書，都以「格林兄弟」之名出版，最後出版的辭典之作者名字，則用「雅哥夫・格林──維爾漢・格林」。雖然兩人的資質不同，但是兩人却如同變成一人一樣地兄弟合作無間。他們共著的「兒童和家庭的童話」是舉世無匹的傑作，這種文學的風格已為舉世公認。

74年8月11日 台灣時報

The Brothers Grimm, Two in One

1. Birth and Education

The Brothers Grimm, Jacob Ludwig Karl Grimm (1785–1863) and Wilhelm Carl Grimm (1786–1859), were German academics, philologists, cultural researchers, lexicographers and authors who together collected and published folklore during the 19th century. Jacob Ludwig Karl Grimm was born on 4 January 1785, and his brother Wilhelm Carl Grimm was born on 24 February 1786. Both were born in Hanau, in the Landgraviate of Hesse-Kassel within the Holy Roman Empire (present-day Germany), to Philipp Wilhelm Grimm, a jurist, and Dorothea Grimm née Zimmer, daughter of a Kassel city councilman. They were the second- and third- eldest surviving siblings in a family of nine children, three of whom died in infancy. In 1791, the family moved to the countryside town of Steinau, when Philipp was employed there as district magistrate (Amtmann). The family became prominent members of the community, residing in a large home surrounded by fields. The children were educated at home by private tutors, receiving strict instruction as Lutherans that instilled in both a lifelong religious faith. Later, they attended local schools.

Their father Philipp died of pneumonia and the family was immediately poverty-stricken. Under the help of their mother's sister, they survived. The brothers left Steinau and their family in 1798 to attend the Friedrichsgymnasium in Kassel, which had been arranged and paid for by their aunt. After graduation from the Friedrichsgymnasium, the brothers attended the University of Marburg. There, the brothers were inspired by their law professor Friedrich von Savigny, who awakened in them an interest in history and philology, and they turned to studying medieval German literature. They shared Savigny's desire to see unification of the 200 German principalities into a single state. Through Savigny and his circle of friends— German romantics such as Clemens Brentano and Ludwig Achim von Arnim—the Grimms were introduced to the ideas of Johann Gottfried Herder, who thought that German literature should revert to simpler forms, which he defined as Volkspoesie (natural poetry) as opposed to Kunstpoesie (artistic poetry).

2. Some Publications.

At the University of Marburg, they began a lifelong dedication to researching the early history of German language and literature, including German folktales. The rise of Romanticism during the 18th century had revived interest in traditional folk stories, which to the Grimms and their colleagues represented a pure form of national literature and culture. In 1811, Jacob published his Uber den altdentschen Meistergesang (Songs of German Maestros in Ancient Times), and Wilhelm put forth a translated work of Heroes' Songs, Folk Tales, and Stories in Ancient Denmark. Both brothers showed interest in German and Germanic ancient literature inspired by Friedrich von Savigny, his law professor at the University of Marburg. The occupation of his country by Napoleon Buonaparte also prompted them to go back to the origins of the ancient culture of the Germanic tribes. Later, they both published the classic collection, Children's and Household Tales (Kinder-und Hausmärchen), which was published in two volumes—the first in 1812 and the second in 1815. Soon later, two volumes of German legends and a volume of early literary history followed. They went on to publish works about Danish and Irish folk tales and Norse mythology, while continuing to edit the German folk tale collection.

The brothers did some jobs before Jacob found full-time employment in 1808 when he was appointed court librarian to the King of Westphalia and went on to become librarian in Kassel. After their mother's death that year, he became fully responsible for his younger siblings. He arranged and paid for his brother Ludwig's studies at art school and for Wilhelm's extended visit to Halle to seek treatment for heart and respiratory ailments, following which Wilhelm joined Jacob as librarian in Kassel. The brothers also began collecting folk tales at about this time, in a cursory manner and on Brentano's request. At this time, they published Deutsche Sagen, 1886-1818. The next year, Jacob published Deutsche Grammatik, where Grimm's law was first discovered. The law is about a systematic sound change, and it led to the creation of historical phonology as a separate discipline of historical linguistics. Jacob continued to collect data in this area and finished two works, Deutsche Rechtsaltertumer, 1828 and Deutsche Mythologie, 1835.

They moved the household to Göttingen in the Kingdom of Hanover where they took employment at the University of Göttingen, Jacob as a professor and head librarian and Wilhelm as professor.

During the next seven years, the brothers continued to research, write, and publish. In 1835, Jacob published the well-regarded German Mythology (Deutsche Mythologie); Wilhelm continued to edit and prepare the third edition of Kinder-und Hausmärchen for publication. The two brothers taught German studies at the university, becoming well-respected in the newly established discipline.

In 1837, they lost their university posts after joining the rest of the Göttingen Seven in protest. The 1830s were a period of political upheaval and peasant revolt in Germany, leading to the movement for democratic reform known as Young Germany. The Grimm brothers were not directly aligned with the Young Germans, but five of their colleagues reacted against the demands of Ernest Augustus, King of Hanover, who dissolved the parliament of Hanover in 1837 and demanded oaths of allegiance from civil servants—including professors at the University of Göttingen. For refusing to sign the oath, the seven professors were dismissed and three were deported from Hanover, including Jacob who went to Kassel. He was later joined there by Wilhelm, Dortchen, and their four children.

To get out of financial difficulties, the brothers planned to edit the book, Deutsche Worterbuch. They calculated that the time they needed to collect data and to finish editing would be more than a century. That means that the book might appear in 1961. In 1840, von Savigny and Bettina von Arnim appealed successfully to Frederick William IV of Prussia on behalf of the brothers who were then offered posts at the University of Berlin. In addition to teaching posts, the Academy of Sciences offered them stipends to continue their research. Once they had established their household in Berlin, they directed their efforts towards the work on the German dictionary and continued to publish their research. Jacob turned his attention to researching German legal traditions and the history of the German language, which was published in the late 1840s and early 1850s; meanwhile, Wilhelm began researching medieval literature while editing new editions of Hausmärchen. Not until they were fifty, did they begin editing the dictionary. In 1854, the first book of it appeared.

After the Revolutions of 1848 in the German states, the brothers were elected to the civil parliament. Jacob became a prominent member of the National Assembly at Mainz. Their political activities were short-lived, as their hope dwindled for a unified Germany and their disenchantment grew. In the late 1840s, Jacob resigned his university position and saw the publication of The History of the German Language (Geschichte der deutschen Sprache). Wilhelm continued at his university post until 1852. After retiring from teaching, the brothers devoted themselves to the German Dictionary for the rest of their lives. Wilhelm died of an infection in Berlin in 1859, and Jacob became increasingly reclusive, deeply upset at his brother's death. He continued work on the dictionary until his own death in 1863.

While at the University of Marburg, the brothers came to see culture as tied to language and regarded the purest cultural expression in the grammar of a language. They moved away from Brentano's practice—and that of the other romanticists—who frequently changed original oral styles of folk tale to a more literary style, which the brothers considered artificial. They thought that the style of the people (the volk) reflected a natural and divinely inspired poetry (naturpoesie) as opposed to the kunstpoesie (art poetry), which they saw as artificially constructed. As literary historians and scholars, they delved into the origins of stories and attempted to retrieve them from the oral tradition without loss of the original traits of oral language.

3. Strong Passions between the Two Brothers

The two brothers are different in personality. Jacob is more rationalistic, while Wilhelm, more literary. Jacob remained single all his life, while Wilhelm was married. This is an interesting contrast; yet, they lived together all their lives. Six of their books in the early period were published signed the two brothers, later ones as Jacob Grimm and Wilhelm Grimm.

The brothers were of different dispositions, and yet they had been working together for their lives and they seem to have been one. Their fairy tales for children and their family have been unparalleled in the world. Their styles have also been widely recognized.

—The Taiwan Times, August 11, 1985.

作者 簡介

■ 沙白，本名涂秀田，一九四四年生，台灣省屏東縣人。屏東初中，台北建國高中畢業，高雄醫學院畢業，日本國立東京大學研究。

■ 沙白自幼年即習中國古典文學，青少年時，更吸取西洋文學和日本文學等，而成為融合中西文學思想的詩人。

■ 曾任現代詩頁月刊主編，阿米巴詩社社長，南杏社長，笠詩社社務委員，心臟詩社社長、布穀鳥詩社同仁、高雄市文藝夏令營講師，亞洲詩人大會和世界詩人大會籌備委員。

■ 曾應邀參加一九八六年漢城亞洲詩人大會，和一九八八年第十屆曼谷世界詩人大會發表論文〈詩是現代社會最重要的空氣〉，獲大會極高評價，曼谷英文大報THE NATION（國民報），以首頁引介此文。一九九〇年長沙世界華文兒童文學會議，艾青作品國際學術研討會。

■ 曾獲中華民國新詩學會詩運獎、高雄市詩歌創作獎、朗誦詩獎、高雄市文藝獎、中華民國兒童文學會獎入圍（第二名獎）、心臟詩獎、柔蘭獎、亞洲詩人大會感謝狀、高雄市牙醫師公會和中華民國牙醫師公會感謝獎、台灣文學家牛津獎候選人。

■ 現任臺一社發行人、《大海洋》詩社社長、中國文藝協會會員、中華民國新詩學會候補監事、世界詩人會會員、世界華人詩人協會創會理事、中華民

- 國兒童文學會會員、台灣省兒童文學會會員、高雄市兒童文學寫作學會理事長、六堆雜誌編委、中華民國牙醫師公會編委。
- 著作：詩集『河品』、詩集『太陽的流聲』、詩集『靈海』、中英文詩集『空洞的貝殼』（余光中、陳靖奇譯）、童詩集『星星亮晶晶』、『星星愛童詩』、童詩集『唱歌的河流』（中華民國兒童文學會獎入圍）、『沙白散文集』、『沙白詩文集』、傳記『不死鳥田中角榮』、『毛澤東隱蹤之謎（補著）』、『牙科知識』、『快樂的牙齒』等，以及T.S艾略特和保羅、梵樂希等英日文學之翻譯和介紹。作品曾被翻譯為英、日、韓文等，在外國及中國大陸曾介紹過。
- 留美：哈佛大學、波士頓大學植牙中心。
- 中華民國口腔植體醫學會專科醫師、台灣牙醫植體醫學會專科醫師、國際口腔植牙專科醫師學會院士、前中華民國口腔植體醫學會監事及專科醫師甄審委員、美國矯正學會會員。
- 國際詩人獎、榮譽文學博士、ABI及IBC國際傑出名人獎、美國文化協會國際和平獎；曾獲兩次國際植牙會議論文第二名獎。
- 沙白詩作列入韓國慈山李相斐博士出版的「現代世界代表詩人選集」。
- 現職：台立牙科診所院長
- 住址：高雄市新興區仁愛一街228號
- 電話：(07)2367603
- 手機：0919180875
- e-mail：shiutientu@gmail.com
- e-mail：taiyi.implant@msa.hinet.net
- 網址：www.taili-dentist.com.tw
- 郵政劃撥：04596534涂秀田帳戶

An Introduction to Tu Shiu-tien (Sar Po)

Born on July 28, 1944 at Toulun Village, Zhutian Township, Pingdong County, Taiwan Province, Republic ofChina.

Education:

Zhutian Primary School, Pingdong;
Provincial Pingdong Middle School;
Jianguo High School, Taipei;
Department of Dentistry, Kaohsiung Medical College.

Foreign institutions where he pursued further studies and research:

Research Institute of Dentistry, National University of Tokyo;
Osaka University of Dentistry;
National University of Osaka;
Research Institute of Dentistry, Harvard University;
Center for Dental Implantation, Boston University.

Interests :

Chinese classics, Western literature, Japanese literature. Oriental and Occidental philosophy and Thoughts on the Arts and their theory.

Honors and Awards :

Award for Writing of Poetry, Kaohsiung.
Award for Chanting of Poetry, Kaohsiung.
Award for the Arts and Literature, Kaohsiung.
Roelan Award, Kaohsiung.
Award from the Society of Cardiology.
Award from the Republic of China Association of New Poetry.
Outstanding prizes from International Poets' Association, ABI (American Biographical Institute) and IBC (International Biographical Center).
Award from the International Society of Poets

A certificate of an academician in the Association of International Dental Implantation Specialists at the University of New York.
Honorary Degree of Doctor of Literature (Litt. D.)
Outstanding People of the 20th-century American Biographical Institute (ABI) and the International Biographical Center (IBC)
Award from the American Cultural Agency for Promotion of World Peace.
Second Award in the presentation of a paper at the International Congress of Oral Implantologists (ICOI), twice.
2004 International Peace Prize, for outstanding achievement to the good of society as a whole, by the authority of the United Cultural Convention sitting in the United States of America.
2005 as one of the Top 100 Writers in Poetry and Literature, witnessed by the Officers of the International Biographical Center at its Headquarters in Cambridge, England.
2005 Lifetime of Achievement One Hundred, signed at the Headquarter of the International Biographical Center of Cambridge, England.

Current Occupation :

Dentist, Taiyi Dental Clinic and Taiyi Dental Implantation Center.

Associations :

President, the Amoeba Poetical Association, Kaohsiung Medical College.
Editor-in-Chief, the Modern Poetry Monthly,
President, the Nanxing Magazine,
President, the Big Ocean Association of Poetry;
A committee member for general affairs, the Li Journal of Poetry;
A lecturer, Kaohsiung Summer Camp;
Associate convener, the section of poetry, Kaohsiung Qingxi Association of the Arts;
Supervisor, the Southern Branch, the Chinese Association of the Arts and Literature;
An editor, the Liudui Magazine;
A preparatory Committee Member, the Asian Poet Conference;
A committee member, the World Olympic Association of Poetry;
An academician, College of World Culture;
Honorary Doctor, World Conference of the Poets.

Classification of His Works:

Collections of Poetry:

Hepin (So. The Streams), Preface by Zhu Chendong, "The Realm of Poetry—a Discussion of Sar Po's Poetry." Taipei: Modern Poetry Club, March 1966.

The Spiritual Sea. Kaohsiung: Taiyi She, September 1990.

The Hollow Shells, with Chinese and English texts, tr. by Yu Guangzhong and Ching-chi Chen. Kaohsiung: Taiyi She, December 1990.

The Streaming Voices of the Sun, in the Collection of Taiwanese Poets, #18, ed. the Li Journal of Poetry. Kaohsiung: Chunhui Publishing Co., November 2019.

Essays on His Poetics:

Sar Po's Essays on His Poetics. Kaohsiung: Chunhui Publishing Co., August 2020.

Prose:

Sar Po's Essays. Taipei: Linbai Publishing Co., September 1988.

Children's Literature:

「星星亮晶晶」Twinkle, Twinkle, Little Stars. Kaohsiung: Taiyi She, October 1986.
「星星愛童詩」Stars Love Children's Poetry. Kaohsiung: Taiyi She, September 1987.
「唱歌的河流」Singing Rivers. Kaohsiung: Taiyi She, September 1990.

Biography :

An Undying Bird, Tanaka Kakuei (不死鳥田中角榮). (In serialization, Taiwan Times.) Tainan: Xibei Publishing Co., May 1984.

Books on Dental Hygiene :

Knowledge on Dentistry. Kaohsiung: Taiyi She, August 1987.
The Happy Teeth. Taizhong: The Commission of Education, Taiwan Provincial Government, April 1993.

Translation of Texts and Theories of literature, Taiwan and Overseas:

"T.S. Eliot, 'The Dirty Salvages'", from English into Chinese, in Sar Po's Essays on His Poetics, pp. 256-273.
"Paul Valery's Literary Theory, One." in Sar Po's Essays on His Poetics, pp. 280-285.
"Paul Valery's Literary Theory, Two." in Sar Po's Essays on His Poetics, pp. 286-294.
"Paul Valery's Literary Theory, Three." in Sar Po's Essays on His Poetics, pp. 295-299.
"Paul Valery's Literary Theory, Four." in Sar Po's Essays on His Poetics, pp. 300-307.
"Paul Valery's Literary Theory, Five." in Sar Po's Essays on His Poetics, pp. 308-312.
"Paul Valery's Literary Theory, Six." in Sar Po's Essays on His Poetics, pp. 313-317.
"Paul Valery's Literary Theory, Seven." in Sar Po's Essays on His Poetics, pp. 318-325.
"On Something about Charles Baudelaire" by Kuritsu Norio, in Sar Po's Essays on His Poetics, pp. 326-336.

"On Charles Baudelaire" by Kuritsu Norio, in Sar Po's Essays on His Poetics, pp. 337-350-349.
"On Charles Baudelaire and His Poetical Language" by Kuritsu Norio, in Sar Po's Essays on His Poetics, pp.350-360.
"On Charles Baudelaire and His Prose" by Kuritsu Norio, in Sar Po's Essays on His Poetics, pp. 361-370.
"On the Pains of Charles Baudelaire" by Kuritsu Norio, in Sar Po's Essays on His Poetics, pp. 371-374.
"On Rambo" by Kuritsu Norio, in Sar Po's Essays on His Poetics, pp. 375-382.
"A Dream Inside and Out, Two Poems," by Shinkawa Kasue, in Sar Po's Essays on His Poetics, pp. 432-433.
"Two Poems by Yamamura Bocho," in Sar Po's Essays on His Poetics, pp. 436-437.
"Some Ideas on Taiwan Poets" by Kaneko Hideo, in Sar Po's Essays on His Poetics, pp. 438-439.
"Kawada Kakuei, Mushanokoji Saneatsu, Chen Tingshi," in Sar Po's Essays on His Poetics. Papers Read in Conferences:

Papers read at the International Conference for Dental Implantation; Presented twice and awarded twice.
"Poetry Is the Most Important Air in Our Modern Society," read at the World Poets' Congress, Bangkok, Thailand, 1988; the speech was published in *The Nation*, Bangkok, Tailand.

譯者 簡介

◨ 陳靖奇
◨ 出生：台灣省雲林縣古坑鄉。
◨ 幼兒園：雲林縣斗六糖廠附設幼兒園。
◨ 國小：雲林縣古坑國民小學。
　　　　台北市西門國民小學。
◨ 初中：台北建國中學。
◨ 高中：台北成功中學。
◨ 學士：國立臺灣師範大學英語學系。
◨ 碩士：國立臺灣師範大學英語研究所。
◨ 博士：美國明尼蘇達大學美國研究所。
　重點研究：美國文學與文化，「二十世紀三零時代的美國左翼文學，
　普羅大眾與資本社會的矛盾等議題。」

◨ 經歷：
　台北市立景美女子高級中學英語科教師。
　私立大同工學院講師。
　國立高雄師範大學教授兼夜間部主任。
　國立高雄師範大學教授兼英語學系主任。
　國立高雄師範大學教授兼英語研究所所長。
　國立高雄師範大學教授兼文學院院長。
　國立空中大學高雄學習中心主任。
　私立和春技術學院教授兼副校長。
　私立致遠管理學院教授兼應用英語學系主任。

Translated by Prof. Ching-chi Chen, Ph.d.

- Born at Gukeng, Yunlin, Taiwan, Republic of China.

■ Educated:

- B.A. and M.A., National Taiwan Normal University, majoring in English.
- Ph.D., University of Minnesota, U.S.A., majoring in American studies (social sciences about America and American literature).

■ Positions held:

- Professor of English, Department of English, National Kaohsiung Normal University.
- Chairperson, the Department of English, National Kaohsiung Normal University.
- Dean, College of the Liberal Arts, National Kaohsiung Normal University.
- Vice President, Hochun Institute of Technology at Daliao, Kaohsiung.

國家圖書館出版品預行編目(CIP)資料

星星亮晶晶 = Twinkle, Twinkle, Little Stars /
沙白著；陳靖奇譯. -- 二版. -- 高雄市：
台一社,民110.09
　面；　公分
中英對照
ISBN 978-626-95122-4-9 (平裝)

863.598　　　　　　　　110015158

Original Chinese text by Sar Po
Translated by Ching-chi Chen, Ph.d.
Published by Shiu-tien Tu
Chinese and English texts copyright 2021 by Shiu-tien Tu
ALL RIGHTS RESERVED

星星亮晶晶
Twinkle, Twinkle, Little Stars

著　　者：沙白 Sar Po
翻　　譯：陳靖奇 Ching-chi Chen, Ph.d.
發 行 人：涂秀田
出　　版：台一社
發 行 所：800高雄市新興區仁愛一街228號
電　　話：886-7-2367603; 886-9-19180875
印　　刷：德昌印刷廠股份有限公司
電　　話：886-7-3831238
郵政劃撥：04596534 涂秀田帳戶
登 記 證：行政院新聞局局版業字第4771號
中華民國七十五年十月廿五日初版
中華民國一一○年九月十五日二版

Email：shiutientu@gmail.com
　　　：taiyi.implant@msa.hinet.net
WWW：TAIYI.egolife.com
　　　：taili-dentist.com.tw

版權所有・翻印必究　　定價新台幣350元(美金15元)